DEMON ASH

M.J. Haag
Becca Vincenza

DEMON ASH

Copyright: M.J. Haag and Becca Vincenza

mjhaag.melisssahaag.com

beccavincenzaauthor.wordpress.com

Published: December 5, 2017

ISBN-13: 978-1-979307-99-4

Cover Design: Shattered Glass Publishing

To our readers who took a chance on something
so uniquely different,
Thank you!

To our readers who were too scared,
The hellhounds are coming for you.

Demon Ash

The world is nothing like Mya remembers. While in Ernisi, cities have been bombed and burned in an attempt to stop the hellhounds and the plague. The survivors are doing everything they can to win back their world from the hell unleashed with the first quake.

With Drav's help, Mya reunites with her family but they are far from safe. Marauders, hellhounds, and the infected are doing their best to destroy what's left of the world, and it's up to Mya and Drav to do their best to save it.

ONE

Everything hurt. The steady throbbing in my skull penetrated my disoriented mind, creating a dark dreamscape filled with terrors I didn't believe real. Skeletal black bodies with glowing red eyes swarmed around us. A single flashlight and four spear-bearing men with grey skin kept them at bay. A man with a mangled face whispered that I would have no second life, that I needed to cling to the first.

I didn't want to cling to anything. Pain enveloped me when I tried. So I let go, but I couldn't drift.

The clamor of sound, echoing howls and incomprehensible shouts, tormented me almost as much as the jolting cadence rocking through my body. I wanted to escape into an abyss of darkness. But every time I came close, something jostled me. Then, the whispers would start again.

The words began to change, along with the light. A brightness crept in that made me whimper and turn my head, despite the pain.

"It's the only safe place," a voice said.

"It will likely house humans," another answered.

I wanted to tell the voices to stop. To be quiet and just let me sleep. But, opening my mouth only produced a mewling whine. Something brushed my forehead, hurting me further.

"Good. They might be able to help her."

"We don't heal the same here. We need to watch for those guns. Do not let them touch you."

"I know," yet another voice said. "You stay. We go."

"Do not kill them. Mya will not like that."

Frustration and confusion got the better of me. I opened my mouth, again, to yell. Nothing more than a groan emerged.

"Shh...my Mya. You are safe. We will find help."

After that, things grew blissfully quiet, and the light faded. I floated in the void of nothing, the pain gradually easing. In its absence, a chill crept in. Even though I couldn't see, I could imagine my breath misting in the air and ice forming on my skin. I shivered uncontrollably, each shudder punctuated by a rapid series of muffled bangs.

"We need to cool her off. She's too warm."

I wanted to cry. Why couldn't the voices just leave me alone? Or say something that made sense. Who would want to cool off when it felt ready to snow?

More pops sounded then silence returned.

"They are angry," a voice said.

Fingers grabbed me with bruising force, and I cried out.

"I don't care," another said. "They will help her. Where are they?"

"Barn. Tied to chairs."

"Take her to the house. Find a bed that is soft. I will be there in a moment. And do not touch her or try to look at her pussy. She will be angry if you do. And so will I."

The rocking started again. I groaned, hating this dream and wishing I could wake up. Instead, I pulled away from the light, the voices, and the pain and found a dark, quiet corner to hide from their persistent presence.

* * * *

Something gently smoothed over my hair, and the warm wetness on my forehead left only to be replaced by a cooler wetness. I sighed and snuggled deeper into the pillow.

"I've sent Ghua back to the hole. He will wait for the others," a familiar voice said.

"Good. What about the ones in the barn?"

"They still only swear and spit at us. Are you sure they are intelligent and not infected?"

"I am sure."

Groaning, I tried to roll away from the voices.

"Shh...Mya. Do not move so much."

"Then shut up," I mumbled.

Arms wrapped around me suddenly and squeezed me too tightly.

"Stop," I panted, my head starting to throb again. "Hurts."

Lips brushed my cheek and the corner of my mouth.

"You're awake," a voice said.

"No." If I was, I sure as hell didn't want to be.

A clank came from nearby. The arm under my shoulders lifted me slightly as something touched my lips.

"Drink, Mya."

I did, gratefully. The water slid down my dry throat. The first swallow hurt, but the ache left by the third gulp.

"Good," the voice said, taking the drink away. "Are you hungry? I have chicken noodle soup."

"No."

The arm eased me back to the bed, and I slept.

* * * *

Awareness came in slow increments. The low murmur of voices. The soft pillow behind my head. The clatter of dishes.

The smell of chicken noodle soup had me opening my eyes. I blinked twice, not sure if I still slept.

Blankets covered the room's two windows, muting the light. I could still see well enough. I lay on a bed in an actual bedroom. A ceiling fan hung above me, its blades unmoving and the light off.

The memories of the last few weeks crawled through my mind. Earthquakes, hellhounds, people becoming infected, looking for my family, finding Drav, the bombings, going to Drav's world. All of it swirled in a confusing jumble until the memories settled and clicked into place to complete a big picture. I'd almost died trying to get to the surface. Not just me. Drav.

A man walked into the bedroom. He bore healing scratches on his face and arms.

"Molev," I said. Panic and worry started to rise. "Where's Drav? Where are we?"

"I'm here," Drav said from behind me. A weight moved on my waist. I reached down and touched his arm under the blankets as I turned my head to look at him.

"We are in a house on the surface," Molev said.

I barely heard. I couldn't stop staring at Drav. He still bore signs of his hellhound attack, but his eyes were no longer swollen, making it easy to see the earnest worry with which he watched me. A scar ran from the top of his left eyebrow, over the bridge of his nose, to his right cheek.

I lifted my hand and gently caressed the new mark. My

eyes watered for what he'd endured to save me and for what I felt for him.

"Hey, handsome," I said softly. "Don't throw me like that again. I thought you'd died."

He leaned forward and pressed a kiss to my temple. I frowned at the vague memory of a dream.

"Did I have a washcloth on my forehead?" I asked.

"Yes. You had a fever."

"Thank you for taking care of me."

"Would you like this soup?" Molev asked, reclaiming my attention. "I warmed it on the stove."

My stomach growled, answering him. I shifted my feet under the covers and wrinkled my nose. They'd tucked me into bed, fully clothed. Shoes and all.

As much as I didn't want to leave Drav or our warm bed, the shoes bothered me.

"How about we go to the kitchen?" I asked.

Molev retreated toward the door as I pulled the covers back and sat up. The abrupt change from laying down to sitting up caused my head to swim, and I waited a moment for the sensation to pass before swinging my legs over the edge of the bed.

"How do you feel?" Drav asked. His warm hand soothed my lower back.

"Weak, but my head doesn't hurt. Ugh! Why do I smell like puke?" I stood and looked down at my stained shirt. I vaguely recalled throwing up during our race from his world.

"Do we still have my bag? I need a new shirt."

"There are some in here," Molev said, opening a door to a small closet.

An assortment of men's button up shirts mixed in with several lady's dresses. Not in a position to be picky, I took one of the long-sleeved dress shirts from the hanger.

"Your bag is here." He pointed to the bag on a nearby chair. "I did not touch your things."

"No one did," Drav said.

"Thanks. Can we meet you in the kitchen?" I asked Molev, hoping he'd get the hint and leave.

He smiled slightly and retreated from the room, taking the mug with him. My stomach rumbled again, and I hurriedly ditched the dirty shirt and put on the clean one. I briefly thought of washing myself up, but just standing was taking more effort than I cared to admit to myself.

Yawning, I went to my bag and checked for my phone. It was there but dead. I pulled out the charger and plugged it in. As soon as I could, I needed to try my brother's number.

When I turned, I found Drav sitting on the edge of the bed and watching me.

"You worried me," he said as he stood.

He wrapped me in a loose hug. The feel of his strong arms gave me a sense of peace. Of safety. I rested my head on his chest and closed my eyes. He held me closer, his hand pressing my lower back so we were flush, front to front. The contact made me shiver and remember our time at the lake. Had that only been a few days ago?

He pressed a kiss to the top of my head and loosened his hold slightly.

"You stopped breathing several times," he said, quietly.

Holy shit.

"I did?" I looked up and met his tormented gaze.

6

"Yes. You moaned and cried once we brought you up here. I wanted to take you back."

"I'm glad you didn't. I do feel better now."

He leaned in and brushed his lips over mine before setting his forehead against mine.

"You are still the best thing here."

His quiet confession made me ache for all the worry he'd endured.

"And you make my heart race in the best way," I admitted.

My stomach growled again. This time he released me fully and took my hand.

"Come. You need to eat."

I almost told him that I'd changed my mind and wanted to go back to bed, but I didn't want him to worry more. Instead, I let him lead me from the room. The short hall led past another bedroom with twin beds. Blankets covered the windows in that room, too, leaving just enough light to see Kerr and Shax each laying on a bed, their eyes closed.

We quietly continued along the hall and down the steps. At the bottom, Drav turned left. I followed a few more steps to the kitchen. My hands shook, and my legs felt weak.

The mug of soup waited on the table along with a multitude of open cans.

"How long have we been here?" I asked as I sank into a seat.

"Several hours."

"That's it?"

I looked at the cans again. Food remained in some of them. Like the can of peas. Others, like the tin of quail eggs and the cans of tuna, were completely empty.

"It looks like you guys ate well."

Molev walked into the kitchen just then, followed by the others I recalled running with Ghua.

"Thank you for keeping me safe and bringing me to the surface," I said.

The men nodded in acknowledgement and continued to watch me.

I lifted the mug of soup and took a sip, not as uncomfortable with their scrutiny as I once had been. My stomach cramped greedily with the first swallow

"This is really good. I needed to eat."

They remained quiet as I consumed the rest of the soup. Once I set the mug aside, Molev sat next to me. I fought to stifle a yawn and lost.

"What's the plan now?" I asked. "Are we safe from the infected and the hellhounds here?" I no longer felt safe in a house after seeing how the hellhounds had brought down the men in the caverns. I looked around the kitchen, wondering what, other than blankets, they'd done to make this place safe for us.

"We wait for the others to join us then help you search for your family," Molev said. "Do you think there are more women who are still healthy like you?"

"I hope so." I yawned again. "How long will it take them to get here?"

"Another day, perhaps. Your skin's color is changing," he said.

The abrupt change in subject had me glancing at Drav. He looked worried as he studied me.

"What do you mean?" I asked.

"It is losing its pinkness," Drav said.

"You mean I look pale?"

"Yes. Very pale."

"Yeah, I think coming downstairs might have been pushing it."

"Then we will return," Drav said. Before I could protest, he picked me up and moved toward the stairs.

"You're limping. I can walk up the stairs on my own. Or have someone else carry me. I don't want you to hurt yourself."

He reached the top step before I finished speaking.

"Stubborn," I mumbled.

"Desperate to hold you."

I set my head against his shoulder and sighed.

"Ditto."

He set me on the mattress, and I quickly kicked off my shoes. I felt a twinge of guilt that we'd messed up the sheets but knew we'd be moving on soon enough anyway, and no one would likely stay in the house again anytime soon. Before I lay down, I checked my phone. It had a charge, but no signal. I hadn't really thought it would. Turning it off, I settled into bed.

Drav snuggled in beside me and covered us.

"Sleep, Mya."

I closed my eyes.

*   *   *   *

When I next woke, the light from behind the blankets had faded considerably. Drav lay beside me, sleeping peacefully. I reached up and gently touched his healing cheek. His fingers twitched over my bra clad breast, and I smiled. Even looking like a homeless woman and smelling faintly of vomit, he wanted me. I melted a little knowing just how much.

Wanting him to rest, I eased from the bed and tucked the covers back around before sneaking from the room.

My growling stomach led me down the hall, past where Shax and Kerr still rested. At the bottom of the steps, I turned to the right and peeked into the living room where Molev lay sleeping on the couch.

As I looked at the fading light sneaking in from behind the blanket covered windows, vague flashes of memory intruded. Images of hounds chasing us and only the flashlight from my bag keeping them at bay. I shook my head and focused on the growing dusk. Night approached, and that meant the hellhounds would return if they were still around. Blanket covered windows wouldn't be enough to keep them out.

The men looked like hell and needed more rest. I could give them another hour before I needed to wake them.

Heading to the kitchen, I jumped in surprise at seeing two fey men sitting quietly at the table, studying closed cans of food.

"Hey, guys," I said quietly. "Are you hungry?"

I reached for one of the cans. Another tin of spam.

"You guys like meat more than the vegetables, so you'll probably like this one." I popped the lid open and handed it over before taking the empty cans to the sink. Underneath, I found a garbage bag and started throwing the trash away while the two men shared the spam. It felt good to move. To do something useful even if there wouldn't be any garbage man to pick the bag up. I figured it didn't hurt to tidy up. Cleaning beat just leaving a mound of used cans on the table for the duration of our stay.

When I finished with the empties, I looked at what remained. The fey hadn't wasted too much. Dumping an assortment of vegetables into a large bowl, I stuck it into the microwave, for the first time noticing the rumble of a generator coming from somewhere outside.

The microwave beeped, and I sat at the table with the guys and started eating the mix of random canned veggies. It didn't taste the best, but given the number of closed cans still on the table top, I wasn't going to be a picky brat. The food was cooked and not going to kill me. Down the hatch it went.

Before I finished, the stairs creaked. Drav's worried gaze found mine.

"Why did you leave?" he asked.

I lifted my spoon. "Hungry."

"You need meat."

"Heck no. I know how you serve up meat."

"I will bring more cans so you can choose something you like."

"That's okay. I'd rather you sit down and tell me what happened since we reached the surface. I think I might have been awake for some of it, but I'm not sure."

He sat in the chair beside me, resting his hand on the back of my neck. His fingers teased my skin as he spoke and I ate.

"We ran north. A pack of the hounds caught up to us just after we left the broken buildings of the city behind. There were too many to keep away with just our weapons and hands, so we used your flashlight until we saw more light in the distance. That light led us here."

"Yeah, I can hear the generator running outside. Were there people here?"

"Yes. Four. With guns."

Surprise lifted my brows, and I struggled to swallow my mouthful of veggies.

"Really? You didn't kill them, did you?" I asked.

"No. They shot at us, but we ignored their challenge and did not remove their heads."

One of the other men said something, and Drav grinned.

"Yes. We are regretting not removing their heads."

"Why? Where are they? I hope you took away their guns."

"The men are tied to chairs in the barn," he answered. "The guns are hidden there with them."

More of my scattered memories solidified. Gunshots. Worried whispers. Swearing.

"I want to talk to them," I said, setting my food aside.

"Are you sure? They usually don't say more than 'fuck off' and spit at us."

I stood. "I'm sure. Let me shower first so they don't mistake me for one of the infected." Other than the clean shirt, I looked like hell. Blood still spattered my jeans.

"Do you need help?" Drav asked, standing.

Although the last time we'd been in the water together had been fun, I knew I didn't have the strength for that.

"Nope. Just my bag."

I expected a frown of disappointment. However, he only nodded and threaded his fingers through mine before leading me back upstairs.

Two

After Drav brought my bag, I closed myself in the nearest bathroom and started the shower. Hot water almost immediately rained down on the old porcelain tub. Eagerly stripping from my clothes, I wrinkled my nose at the dirty spot on the top of my foot.

"You're so nasty," I said to myself.

I opened the linen closet and grinned. A stack of wrapped toothbrushes, razors, and new deodorants sat next to bottles of shampoo, boxes of bar soap, and tubes of new toothpaste. Way too many of the same kind of supplies neatly stacked together to belong in a normal house.

Leave it to Drav to find the home of some kind of prepper. Shaking my head, I grabbed a razor, toothbrush, and toothpaste.

The shower felt like heaven. Water beat down on me, washing away the remaining aches. I soaped my hair, then scrubbed every inch of my body. The mark on the top of my foot didn't come off. I figured it might be a bruise, but it didn't really hurt. Shrugging it off, I shaved then rinsed.

By the time I finished, I felt like a new person and grinned at myself in the mirror until I noticed a mark near my collar bone. It appeared to be the same greyish purple as the one on the top of my foot and, like the other spot, didn't hurt when I pressed on it. I dried, did a slow turn in front of the mirror, and found another spot on my lower back.

"Drav?" I called.

"Do you want me to come in?" he asked from the other side of the door.

I wrapped the towel around my torso before saying yes. When he entered, his gaze swept over me, lingering on the exposed parts. I could feel myself flush, and my stomach danced distractingly. I let my gaze sweep over the grey skin of his familiar face. The healing scars didn't change my level of attraction one bit. I still wanted him for keeps.

"I have something weird to ask. Can you put your hand by my foot?"

He immediately squatted down and did as I asked. When he looked up at me—well, not quite at me, more like my crotch—his gaze heated. Before I could say anything, he pressed a kiss to my exposed knee. My concern about the grey patches of skin faded as a tingle spread. He kissed my thigh, right where towel and skin met, then buried his face in the towel over the V of my legs.

My knees went weak, and I gripped the sink with one hand.

"Was this just to get me close to your pussy? Can I kiss it again?" he said, pulling back to look up at me.

"Geez!" I clapped a hand over his mouth. "Can you stop saying that word?"

"Kiss?" he questioned, the word muffled by my hand.

"No. And I'm not saying it. And no, I wasn't asking you to squat down so we could make out. I'm not sure I've recovered enough for that."

His hand snaked up the outside of one leg and back down again, tempting me beyond belief to reconsider. I cleared my throat and focused.

"I'm worried, Drav. Look at your hand and that spot on my foot. They look close to the same color, don't they?"

He glanced down again and rubbed his thumb over the mark before meeting my gaze.

"They do."

"That's what I thought. I think I was changing, like you had, but wasn't strong enough. Maybe because I have no magic. I don't know. But, I do know I was dying. No matter what, I can't go back down to your caves. I think I got out just in time."

Drav frowned, his thumb sweeping over my skin again and again.

"We will not go back," he vowed.

I smiled slightly.

"Thank you. Do you want to shower while I get dressed?"

Before I even finished, he stood and dropped his pants.

"You are shameless," I said, looking my fill. "Not that I'm complaining."

He leaned down and kissed me gently. My heart fluttered, and I lifted my hand to his shoulder to steady myself. A puckered bit of skin under my fingers had me pulling back instead of pressing in for more. Dirt and grime covered him as much as it had me. And blood. A lot of dried blood.

"Get cleaned up. I'll be waiting for you in the bedroom."

Only after I said the words did I realize how they might sound. He stepped into the shower, his hot gaze not releasing me until he closed the curtain and turned on the water.

With a deep calming breath, I picked up my bag and, in just the towel, left the bathroom. Molev saw me in the hallway, his curious gaze traveling the length of me.

"Not happening, Molev," I said. "Towel stays on."

He chuckled and stepped into Kerr and Shax's room while I entered the one I'd shared with Drav. Seeing Molev had helped remind me of the task at hand. I needed to talk to the men the fey had in the barn. Dusk was falling, and I didn't know how safe we were here.

After closing the door, I dug in my bag, looking for a fresh pair of underwear and a clean pair of jeans. Fate spared me with the underwear, but not the jeans. I took what I could get, found a pair of sweats in one of the dressers and a t-shirt in another. Still looking like a hobo, but a clean one, I gathered up my clothes and went in search of a washer, hoping we would be able to stay long enough to use it. If not, I'd raid houses along the way.

When I finished, I returned to the bedroom and found Drav dressed and waiting for me.

"Ready?" he asked.

I nodded and squeaked when he scooped me up into his arms.

"I can walk," I said.

"Yes. But I like carrying you."

"Yeah, I know. Cuz I jiggle."

He pressed a soft kiss to my lips that made me yearn for more.

"And I don't want you to lose your pink coloring again," he said.

He left the room and carried me downstairs. With Molev, Shax, and Kerr close behind, we left the house.

Dusk had already come and gone. The brightness from several portable stadium-type lights, which I'd mistaken for daylight, illuminated the fenced-in yard and barn. Curled barbed wire topped the chain link fence, and I shivered.

This wasn't the home of a prepper. This went way beyond prepping. The people who owned this place were not messing around. The additional height of the barbed wire above the fence brought the top close to level with the second story windows. Definitely taller than normal. Hopefully, the fence and the light would be enough to keep the hellhounds out.

Drav stepped over to the large, red-painted barn. Deep furrows marked the boards facing the house. Hellhounds. Shit. I hoped that was before the fence and lights went up.

"You put the humans in here? You didn't hurt them, did you?" I asked.

"No. They would like to kill us and challenge us continually. We've ignored them and kept them safe for you but are willing to accept their challenge if you are not against the idea," Molev said.

Whoever had been here first had really rubbed the fey the wrong way.

"I'm against it."

"You can let me down, Drav. I promise on the way back you can carry me."

Drav grunted but set me down as Kerr and Shax stepped forward to open the large door. Enough of the light filtered in to reveal a large filled space. It wasn't until I fully entered that I understood what type of place the fey had found. Not a home of hoarders or preppers but a secured location for a group of looters.

Pallets and racks full of supplies created two columns of aisles extending into the shadowy depths of the building. My eyes widened as I walked over to the nearest pallet of neat layers of bathroom supplies stacked one on top another. My thoughts went back to my shower and all the supplies in that cupboard.

Wood scraped against the floor, drawing my attention to the four men tied to chairs just inside the door. Based on appearances, they ranged in age from Ryan to my dad. All four watched us with varying levels of fear and hostility. I couldn't blame them. They didn't know Drav's people and being tied to chairs by them certainly didn't make a good impression.

"Hi," I said.

One man curled his lip back in distaste while the rest of them remained silent. I stepped closer, and Drav reached out to stop me from approaching the men.

"No, Mya."

"It's okay."

He didn't seem convinced but released his gentle hold on my arm. I moved toward the men, giving them a friendly smile. One turned his head away, refusing to look at me.

"I'm trying to find my family. We lived in Oklahoma. I was away at university when the hellhounds attacked. I got one call from my brother in the brief window when they turned on communications for the bombing warnings. He said my family had been evacuated to a safe zone, but he didn't know where. I need to find them."

The man in front of me scooted back in his chair, sitting a

little straighter. A surge of hope grew inside of me. His lips twisted before he opened his mouth and spat at me.

Drav picked me up and moved me further back, growling a warning at the man.

"Challenge her again, and you will deal with me," Drav warned.

The man scowled at us but remained quiet.

"Please," I said, trying again. "Where are the safe zones?"

"Fuck off, slut," one said.

That's why they were spitting at me? Because I was with the fey?

"You fuckers brought back those damned hounds," another said hotly. "The bombing nearly wiped them out."

Guilt nipped at me. The bombings had successfully driven the hounds from the surface. Yet, herding them back to Ernisi wasn't any fairer to the fey than siccing the hounds on the humans.

"The hounds would have returned no matter what." I glanced at the supplies crowding the inside of the building. "This can't all be just for you. Please, tell us where we can find a safe zone. These guys can help with the hounds."

"Help with the hounds?" the one who'd spit sneered. "Like the two who helped drive the infected in here?"

"What two?" I asked, glancing at Drav.

The rude man on the chair made a sound of disgust.

"Get a little demon cock, and you think they can help?" he said. "They're all the same. Killers. It's better to die than to let one of them touch you."

Anger flushed my cheeks. I understood the men were scared and lashing out with their crude words, but knowing that didn't make them any less hurtful.

"You're going after the wrong people, here. I'm not the enemy. These guys aren't the enemies. The hellhounds spreading the disease that created the infected are the real enemies."

"If these guys aren't the enemy, then why are we tied up?" the younger one asked, a slight quaver in his voice.

"Because you shot at them. They aren't stupid. They know you'd do it again in a heartbeat, given the chance."

"Damn straight, demon whore. We know our side," the older one said.

Drav's grip around my waist tightened, and his free hand curled into a fist.

"What is the point of all this slut shaming and name calling? What do you think it's going to accomplish? You're wasting time and proving you're an asshole. That's it."

"You are changing colors again, Mya," Molev said. "Maybe it's time for you to return indoors and rest some more."

I debated leaving. So far, the men had acted exactly as Drav and Molev had said. All they did was spit and curse. I couldn't force them to talk. Letting them calm down seemed like the smarter thing to do. Hopefully, they would see the fey men posed no threat, given time.

"You're right," I said to Molev. "I should rest."

Before Drav could pick me up, a new sound rose over the rumble of the generator. The oldest man stilled, and a smile crossed his lips at the roar of an approaching engine. A tingle of worry erupted in my stomach.

"Are there more of you?" I asked.

He continued to smile slightly and remained silent.

Turning my back on the bound men, I went to the barn entrance where Shax was standing. I was glad he made it out of the caverns whole, his hair still intact.

I patted his arm and smiled up at him as I walked past.

"Mya, it might not be safe," Drav said from right behind me.

Outside, a big black truck idled on the other side of the gate. My heart slammed in my chest at the sight of a shadowy, long line of people further down the road. The mass moved with single-minded purpose toward the truck. Infected. The idea of a truck full of more gun-toting humans did worry me, but not as much as leaving the humans to fend for themselves outside the gate with those oncoming infected.

I opened my mouth to say we needed to let the truck in when the driver's door swung outward. My mouth stayed open at the sight of Ghua as he walked toward the fence and unlocked it.

"Good. Ghua has returned with the others," Drav said from behind me.

Without preamble, Drav lifted me in his arms and began moving toward the house. I twisted to look at the people still on the road. They didn't stagger and waver like the infected.

Ghua saw me, raised a hand in greeting, then got back into the truck. It rumbled forward up the drive.

"Can you put me down?"

"You said I could carry you back," Drav said, shifting my weight in his arms.

"Yeah, but I want to talk to Ghua. I want to know what it's like out there."

"Barren, except for infected and hounds," Drav answered

without stopping. "The men will be tired from traveling in the sun for hours. You can talk to them after they rest."

With the truck out of the way, the fey wearily filed into the yard. My heart squeezed at the sight.

"Tired and probably hungry," I said. "I'm betting that barn has a lot of soup. After you drop me off inside, can you go back for a few cases? Soup will be quick and easy to heat up."

Drav nodded and set me down inside of the house. While I searched for pots in the kitchen, he left to get the food. Molev, Shax, and Kerr came in before he returned.

"Thank you for thinking to feed them, Mya," Molev said. "They are tired from making their way out of Ernisi with the remaining hellhounds chasing after them."

I placed four pots on the stove. It had looked like at least forty men following behind the truck.

"No problem. Can you two go help Drav with the soup? I'm guessing we'll need a lot."

Molev nodded to Shax and Kerr. Those two left, and he sat at the table. A few moments later, the kitchen door opened again, followed by heavy footfalls.

With a wide smile on his face, Ghua stepped into the room. He looked untouched from the hellhound attacks but still tired and dirty.

"Food then rest," Molev said. "Sit and tell us the news while you wait to eat."

Ghua sat, and I went to get him a glass of water. He thanked me, drained the cup, then looked at Molev.

"The hounds have abandoned the crater. That is a good thing for the men who still need to leave the city. They have divided into three more groups. A group of ten is waiting in the old orchard to direct the others to our location. As you asked, a group will remain behind to guard the city."

Molev grunted in acknowledgement. I inhaled, ready to ask Ghua where the heck he'd learned so much English, but the arrival of Drav, Kerr, and Shax with cases of canned soup distracted me. Directing the men to set the cases on the table, I began sorting the cans while Ghua continued.

"Twice while waiting, I saw a lone human. The first one stayed back as if afraid to approach. However, when I went to greet it, I could smell the decay and see the wounds from a hound. The second ran before I could tell if it was one of the intelligent ones or not."

"It sounds like the bombs really did decrease the infected numbers if you only saw two," I said, removing anything tomato based or with peas from the variety of soups they'd brought.

"Yes, in the cities. But, not outside of them. We killed many groups of infected on the way here. The lone sightings were different."

Drav helped me open the cans. I dumped all the chicken based soups into a separate pot from the beef based ones and turned the heat all the way up.

"Any injuries?" Molev asked.

"Yes. Dax and Tor were hurt. Hound injuries from the caverns. They had reached the surface shortly after us. I found them when I went back. They slept in the bed of the truck, under a cover, while we waited."

"They will heal," Drav said, catching the sidelong look I gave his injuries. "So will I."

"I know. The soup is almost ready."

"Ghua, let the men know to come in. They can rest anywhere inside the house, except the bed in the last bedroom. That is for Mya and Drav."

Blushing, I walked away to change over the laundry while listening to Ghua leave. I added a dryer sheet and started the machine, grateful for the generator, before returning to the stove.

Ghua walked back into the kitchen a short while later followed by the first of the men who'd traveled with him.

Once the soups were warm, I pulled out dishes from the cabinets and began ladling out portions. Drav set the first two servings in front of Molev and Ghua before coming back for his own.

Cup in hand, I ladled another serving and swayed unexpectedly on my feet. Drav was right there to steady me.

"You need to rest," he said.

I nodded and handed the cup off to one of the men waiting for his portion.

Drav lifted me into his arms and pressed his lips against my forehead. I set my head on his chest and let him take me upstairs.

THREE

Drav's fingers stroked the skin of my stomach, waking me. Feeling much better than the day before, I snuggled closer and smiled sleepily as his hand drifted lower. Movement on the floor beside our bed reminded me we weren't alone, though. I grabbed his wrist as I opened my eyes and shook my head at him.

He exhaled heavily but stopped his tempting assault. Mutually disappointed, I gave him a quick kiss on the cheek and quietly sat up. At least ten men had found space to sleep on the floor.

Ghua lay right beside the bed on my side. He opened his eyes and looked up at me then winked. I shook my head and tossed a pillow down at him.

"Don't get weirder," I whispered. "Skootch over so I can tip-toe out of here."

Half the men in the room opened their eyes and sat up.

"Sorry." I quickly stood and made a beeline for the door. Drav followed closely behind.

When I glanced back, I saw Ghua move from the floor to my spot in bed. I couldn't blame him. Sleeping on the floor sucked.

In the hall, I stepped around more bodies. Some fey even

leaned on the stairs. There were far more men present this morning than there had been when Drav had taken me upstairs. They lay in any open spot. Even in the kitchen. Those who slept in there stirred as soon as I entered the room.

I motioned for Drav to follow me outside and felt bad when his eyes began to water in the early morning light.

"I was thinking I could cook something for everyone. Or at least try to. How many men do you think are here? A hundred?"

"At least."

"Come on. Let's see what we can find in the barn."

Before we even made it halfway across the yard, I heard muffled yells from within the building and hurried my steps. Drav beat me to the door and went through with a growl. I peeked around him and almost laughed.

The four men still sat in their chairs, but gags now stuck from their mouths. The one on the right rocked from side to side, his face beat red in his agitation.

"Hey, guys," I said to the fey standing guard. "What's going on?"

The human men all started yelling behind their gags, and one of the fey began speaking to Drav. Walking up to the rude guy who'd spit at me yesterday, I pulled the gag from his mouth.

"I'm going to fucking shit my pants," he yelled at me.

"Yeah, that wouldn't be cool."

I looked at one of the nearby fey.

"What's your name?" I asked him.

"Anizo, Mya."

"Anizo, will you please untie this man—"

26

"My name's Bud, bitch."

"—and take him outside so he can relieve himself?"

"Yes," Anizo said.

I turned away from the pair and found Drav glaring at the man who'd just called me a bitch.

"It's not worth getting angry over, Drav. They're scared, and they don't understand. Honestly, tying them to chairs isn't going to help win them over either."

"Nothing you do will win us over, you grey-skinned piece of shit," Bud said with venom.

"For Pete's sake." I turned on the man. "Did you like the gag in your mouth? Do you want to crap your pants? Do yourself a favor and shut your pie hole." I looked at Anizo. "After Bud's done, take the rest outside, too. Don't retie them, but keep a close eye on them." I studied the dirty human men. "If you want, come inside, clean yourselves up, and get something to eat. Do yourselves a favor, though, and stay away from any form of weapon. The fey will see it as a challenge. And, trust me, you'll lose if they decide to take you up on what they perceive as a challenge."

Shaking my head at their continued angry glares, I moved down the aisle of racks until I found one with boxes of mac and cheese.

"Don't touch our fucking food, demon whore," one of the men yelled.

I heard a slight thump of flesh on flesh and shook my head again.

"Idiot," I mumbled under my breath. No doubt, Drav had hit the man. I just hoped he'd held back a little.

Grabbing one of the nearby laundry baskets, I knocked at

least fifty boxes of mac and cheese in, then went to look for the spam and tuna fish. Once I had a full basket, I joined Drav, who stood at the end of the aisle, watching the men slowly walk around. Two of them were standing close and whispering.

"Don't be stupid," I said, moving toward the door. "Because the fey aren't."

Outside the barn, Drav took the basket from me.

"Why can we not remove their heads?" he asked, his tone indicating sincere puzzlement.

"Because there are so few healthy humans left. Because you guys aren't cruel and know now head removal would result in a final death."

Neither of those reasons seemed to be an answer for Drav.

"Because I'm asking you not to," I added.

He grunted, and I grinned.

In the kitchen, those who had been sleeping now milled about. One said something to me that I couldn't understand. I looked to Drav to translate.

"He's wondering if he can help."

I nodded. Others offered to help too, creating the whole "too many cooks in the kitchen" scenario. Not wanting to hurt anyone's feelings but needing to create some space to work, I came up with another idea.

"Actually, I have a different task for anyone willing."

They moved aside as I made my way to the television in the living room. As I'd hoped, a shelf of DVD cases hung from a wall. The titles ranged from kids' classics to adult action films. Selecting one that looked like it would have plenty of words and a family friendly rating, I went to the TV.

The number of men who had crowded into the room made

28

maneuvering a little cozy. Molev now sat up on the couch, freeing additional space for others.

"This," I said, holding up the DVD, "will help you all learn some English." They quietly watched me put the DVD into the player and turn on the television.

"Only I am allowed to change the movie," I said, straightening.

"Why?" Molev asked.

"Movies can be different things. Some are real, but most, like the ones in this house, are make-believe. The only human you've ever really known is me. That means, so far, my behavior has been the sole basis of your opinion of humans. Some of these movies have humans pretending to do things most humans would never do. We're not going to have an easy time convincing the rest of my kind how good you guys really are. And, I don't want you watching stuff that will have you giving up on the humans before you give them a chance. Because I don't want you to get the wrong ideas about us, I don't want you to watch those kinds of movies. Make sense?"

"Yes," Molev said. The rest echoed him.

"Now, get comfy. Most movies last between an hour and a half to two hours. This one has a lot of pretending in it, but not bad stuff. It's more silly than anything. If you see or hear something that doesn't make sense or seems unbelievable, ask me about it. By the time this is done, I should have something ready for everyone to eat."

Just as I finished speaking, Bud came walking in with Anzio. He glared at me and went to stomp off in the direction of the bathroom.

"Door stays open," I said. "No razors. Just the soap. And

if Anzio doesn't trust you, he'll probably open the curtain. You'll get used to it."

Bud mumbled something under his breath and kept going, Anzio close on his heels. I started the movie, which was about a father who accidentally shrunk his children, before going back to a much emptier kitchen. Drav stood by the stove, staring at two large kettles of steaming water.

"Is this right?" he asked.

"Yep. Next, we start opening these boxes."

With the help of a few others, we had a meaty version of mac and cheese ready to feed the multitudes by the time the movie finished.

Molev joined us in the kitchen and waited for me to scoop out three bowls. I handed one to him, one to Drav, and kept one for myself, understanding their routine now. We sat at the table and ate while the rest of the men slowly filed into the kitchen. The ones with the shortest hair stood by the sink and washed plates as the others finished.

Drav, Molev, and I took our time.

"If the humans here don't know where the safe zones are, we'll need to find them on our own," I said to Molev. "I doubt we'll find another setup like this, though. Safety from the hounds...a lot of food..."

He nodded thoughtfully.

"They mentioned two others of our kind," Drav said to Molev.

"You think those are the two who killed the man in your world?" I asked.

Molev let out a long breath. "Yes. It is unfortunate they have not given into a final death up here. We will watch for them as we search for your safe zones."

"The hellhounds and infected will make traveling at night harder with a large group of men and you," he said. "Perhaps we send scouts out during the day. They can look for other humans and report back before nightfall."

"That's a good idea," I said. "We can keep playing movies so the ones who leave will be able to talk a little. Not all humans are jackasses like the ones you found here."

"I heard that, bitch," a voice yelled from somewhere beyond the kitchen. The yell was immediately followed by a solid thump.

"Remember you guys are stronger than humans when you hit him," I called out. "Don't break bones. It's not fair."

"Yes, Mya," a voice returned.

A moment later, Bud walked into the kitchen. The pissed off look on his face hadn't mellowed with his shower.

"Come sit," I said.

He opened his mouth to respond but closed it again when every fey in the room stopped what they were doing to look at him.

Sullenly, he sat in the fourth chair.

"Where are you from, Bud? Around here?"

"I'm not answering any of your questions."

"Why not? You've already proven what an asshole you are. No one is going to contest that. And the answers you have aren't any kind of state secret. I'm just trying to figure out what I missed in the last week or so. How bad were the bombings? Are there any cities left? Any hope for us survivors to rebuild our lives?"

He snorted.

"Rebuild? What do you think you're going to see in your lifetime? A shopping mart open on the street corner? That's not going to happen. That world is dead."

I nodded slowly, understanding what he meant.

"Yeah. It is. How many of us are left?"

"I'm not telling you that."

I rolled my eyes.

"Probably because you don't know. I saw a bunch of guys like you on a bridge north of Oklahoma City. The douchecanoes were taking supplies from people still leaving. Is that how you got all your supplies? Jacking other people's stuff?"

"Hell, no. We cleaned out the evacuated town ten miles from here. Lost two guys to the infected before the bombing. Another one to the two grey-skinned fuckers that came after."

"I'm sorry. They aren't with this group."

He snorted in response to that.

"Are there less infected now, after the bombing?"

"Shit no. At least not that we can tell. Out here isn't so bad, but we still see them on supply runs." He got quiet for a minute, looking down at the table. I waited and was rewarded when he looked up at me with just a pinch less anger in his gaze.

"Our men should have been back by now. If you're sending these guys out, I want to go and look for them."

"Honestly, that would be helpful. But, you wouldn't get a gun or any other kind of weapon. Do you still want to go?"

The anger returned.

"Do you think I'm some kind of idiot? I'll die out there with nothing."

"I haven't had a weapon since this started. Do I look

dead?"

He glared at me and looked pointedly at my boobs. Drav growled beside me.

"He wasn't looking at me with interest," I said, patting his hand. "He's hinting that you guys have only kept me safe because I'm a girl, which is true." I focused on Bud again. "That also means they will keep you safe because I'm asking them to. Well, safe as long as you don't do something that puts them in danger."

"Why do you love them so damn much?" the man asked with contempt.

"Haven't you figured it out yet? Beyond the fact that they're actually nice, they are our only hope against those hellhounds. Have you ever seen one die? No," I said answering for him. "Because they're that hard to kill. But these guys know how to fight them without dying themselves."

At least, I hoped they did.

FOUR

"Fine. I'll go," Bud said.

After that, I listened to Molev give orders, in English, to the men who wanted to go out.

"Hey, Bud, would you happen to have a dozen pair of sunglasses?"

He stared at me like I was insane. I held his gaze until he relented.

"We might have some," he said.

"Good." I looked at the nearest fey men. "Can you bring Bud out to the barn? He will show you where to find the glasses. They'll help with the sunlight."

The fey who were willing to scout for the day led Bud through the kitchen door. I stood and pulled back the blanket to watch them through the window. Bud's friends were being escorted to the house. The two groups stopped for a minute as the humans spoke to each other. I nibbled at my lip, uncomfortable with the mistrust swelling inside me.

Bud and his friends could plot all they wanted, and it wouldn't likely do any good. But, the fact they still wanted to plot sucked. That meant we weren't doing a very good job of finding any common ground. I wished I would have been awake when we'd arrived. The tension would have been lower by now if the men hadn't spent a day and a night tied to chairs.

The human men looked at the house then back to Bud and nodded before they resumed walking toward the house.

"We should tell the scouts to watch for a new, safe place further north of here," I said, returning to my chair. "We'll need to keep moving as we look for the safe zones. I think staying in one place for too long will be dangerous."

Molev grunted in agreement just before the men entered. The youngest of them immediately glanced at the small portion of leftover food in the pot on the stove.

"You're welcome to it. Or you guys can make something else if you want. Shower. Use the toilet. Do whatever you need to do." I hoped my offer to let them in the house would help gain their trust.

The men didn't say anything, but one separated from the rest and went to the bathroom. The other two stood near the sink, considering the leftover food.

"What are your names?" I asked.

"Fuc—"

Molev and Drav growled. The fey watching the movie in the living room grew very silent.

"Might want to watch your language," I said. "They understand."

"I'm Jerry," the silent, younger one finally said.

The guy with the sailor mouth glared at the kid.

"Learn to keep your mouth shut," he growled.

The third human returned to the kitchen, and sailor mouth left the room in a temper.

"Friendly," I said with an eye roll. "I'm Mya." My hope to start willing introductions was rewarded.

"Tucker," the new arrival said.

"And your friend with the temper?"

"Butch."

"Thanks. Is there anything you can tell me about other survivors?"

Jerry and Tucker exchanged looks. When both remained silent, I stood up from the table.

"Think about it. I have to change over the movie."

Drav stood and walked with me to the living room. Most of the fey were sneaking glances at the guys in the kitchen. While I protected the fey from negative influence with the movie choices, there wasn't much I could do about real life negative influences. And, I hated that.

Plucking another movie off the shelf, I faced the men crowding the living room.

"Any questions so far?"

"Is there really a machine that will shrink people?" one asked.

"No. Not that I know of."

"Do all married people have children?" another asked.

"No. Some choose not to."

"Will you and Drav have children?"

"Okay. Time for the next movie," I said quickly, turning around once more to change the disk out.

Just as I moved toward Drav, Butch stepped out of the hall from the bathroom and bumped into me. I stumbled a step. Drav steadied me with an arm around my waist at the same time something thudded.

I glanced up to see one of the fey pressing Butch into the wall. Butch's eyes widened further as the gray fist wrapped around his t-shirt and lifted him to the point his toes barely touched the floor.

"Ease up," I said. "It was an accident."

The fey didn't step back. I absently brushed away Drav's hold and went to the fey.

"It was just an accident," I repeated. "Not a challenge or a disrespect or whatever. No harm done, I promise."

The fey reluctantly released Butch. From the look he gave the man, the fey still itched for a fight.

"Go join the others in the kitchen," I said to Butch.

Butch glanced at me, then the fey I had coaxed off of him, before nodding and heading to the kitchen.

"Mya? What is this?"

I turned toward the unfamiliar voice to find an almost bald fey holding up a clean pair of my underwear.

"I took it from the machine that stopped making noise," he said.

I snatched the garment out of his hand, fighting not to turn red. Drav watched me closely, probably trying to determine if the fey had upset me. The last thing I needed was more man-drama, though. So when I answered, I kept my tone free of the annoyance and embarrassment I felt.

"That's my laundry. Thank you for letting me know it's dry."

The fey nodded and retreated to the kitchen. Drav frowned after the man.

"I'm going to go upstairs and put my stuff away. I'll be back down in a bit. Keep an eye on things for me and make sure there's no fighting," I said to Drav, but the entire room answered with a "yes, Mya."

I grabbed my laundry from the dryer down the hall then went upstairs. With the departure of the scouts and the movie playing, I found our bedroom blissfully empty. Exhaling slowly, I closed the door and pulled the blankets off the windows.

Sunlight streamed into the room and warmed my skin. I stood there, looking out without really seeing the barren trees beyond the backyard's fence. The impossibility of the task before me weighed heavily on my shoulders. How would the fey and humans ever find common ground?

If the vision I had was true, the fey had as much right to this world as the humans, if not more. Although the release of the hellhounds had caused the zombie apocalypse, the fey weren't to blame. At least, not these fey. And, we couldn't even fully blame their ancestors. Our damn mining broke the barrier and released the creatures the exiled fey had inadvertently created. I saw the injustice in all of it, but would the rest of my race?

After a moment, I became aware of my idle staring at the woods, and my gaze shifted to the right. My stomach plummeted when I saw something other than a tree. The woman dressed in a torn, dark brown business suit almost blended with the surrounding barren forest. The mangled stump of her right hand pressed against the nearest trunk as she stood there. The utter stillness of the infected sent a shiver of fear racing down my spine. She reminded me of the woman stuck in her seatbelt, waiting for someone to get close enough. This one waited just outside the fence. How long had she been standing there? Had removing the blankets from the window caught her attention?

"Drav?" I called.

The sound of my voice seemed to startle the infected because she took off running. I frowned. They'd never done that before. Noise always drew them closer.

Feet pounded on the stairs.

"What's wrong, Mya?" Drav said, stepping into the room.

"There was an infected outside. Just there," I said, pointing.

I'd barely finished speaking before three fey came into view in the backyard. I pushed the window open and directed them to the spot where she'd stood.

"She was on the other side of the fence. Standing there. Not moving, just staring up at me."

One of the fey remained where she'd been while the other two disappeared. I watched a group of fey search the other side of the fence until Drav pulled me away from the window.

"You are safe, Mya. Let's go downstairs."

"I know I'm safe. It was just really creepy."

"You always find them creepy."

I did, but this time felt different.

We waited in the nearly empty living room with the movie paused. Molev said nothing until the majority of the men returned.

"What did you find?" he asked.

One of the original three stepped forward.

"We found an infected and took his head off. He wasn't alone. There were other tracks. We did not follow those."

"There is no need if they are outside the fence," Molev said.

Before my thoughts could linger on the whole incident, a commotion broke out in the kitchen. I hurried through the door to find a fey and Butch glaring at each other. Kerr's restraining hand on the fey's shoulder had probably saved Butch's life, by the looks of things.

"What happened?" I asked.

"This demon-fuck tried to attack me," Butch said.

"No, Mya," the fey said with an earnest glance in my direction.

"Butch, you obviously did something that challenged him in some manner," I said.

"No, I didn't," he snapped a little too quickly.

"He insulted you, Mya," the fey said.

Behind me, Drav growled. I raised my brow at that but didn't scold him or the other fey. Their protectiveness warmed me.

"He is fucking lying," Butch said.

"Watch your language," I said too late as the fey lunged forward again.

"Stop!"

The men all froze and looked at me. Drav stepped forward and wrapped a protective arm around my waist. No doubt, if the fighting continued, I'd find myself upstairs in the bedroom before I could blink.

"We really need to find a more peaceful way to resolve issues that arise. Molev, I get that your way involves death-match challenges, but you understand why that won't work on the surface, right?"

"Yes," he agreed, giving the fey a hard look.

The man stopped trying to go after Butch, but his open hostility remained. I sighed, wracking my brain for another option.

"Arm wrestling," I said suddenly with a wide smile. "It'll be perfect."

"Are you serious?" Butch said. "What the hell is that going to prove?"

"It's physical and pits the strength of the two opponents against each other. Their current way of handling disputes is to see who can rip the other person's head off first. You want to try that?"

He glared at me. Ignoring him, I focused on his companions.

"Um…Jerry? Tucker? Do you mind showing them what arm-wrestling is while I explain?"

The two men stepped over to the table and sat down. They rested their elbows on the surface and clasped hands. All the fey paid close attention as both men strained for a moment before Tucker's arm gave way and slammed against the table.

"The object of the challenge is to overpower your opponent using only the strength in your arm. If you rip off your opponent's arm, you lose. If you make your opponent bleed or break any bones, you lose."

Butch snorted, obviously not believing either of those scenarios a possibility. For a brief moment, I wished I hadn't said anything and let him find out for himself. However, that wouldn't help the whole demon-human relations thing I was trying to fix.

I continued as if I hadn't heard him.

"If your hand touches the surface first, you lose. If your elbow leaves the table, you lose. And you can't pull your opponent's elbow from the table, either. That's cheating, and you'd lose. The only way to win is what they just demonstrated. Any questions?"

No one spoke up.

"Okay, this will replace your death challenges while you are up here. And, not just against humans," I said with a glance at Molev, "but against each other."

Molev nodded his agreement.

The fey, who'd heard Butch talking about me, took the seat Tucker had abandoned and motioned to Butch. Butch glared but took a seat as well. I could see the determined glint in his eye. He wanted to best the fey. I felt bad knowing I'd set him up with an impossible task. The pair clasped hands like Jerry and Tucker had demonstrated.

Drav's fingers brushed against my skin just under the side of my shirt. I leaned back against him, hoping the fey would use caution with the humans.

Butch glared at his opponent, and it wasn't until I saw the vein in Butch's forehead pop out that I realized they had already started. The fey looked bored and glanced over at me, as if wondering if he should begin. I nodded. He smiled, his fangs flashing, and slammed Butch's hand down on the table. Butch looked dazed, then his face turned red.

"Rematch. I demand a rematch."

The growing heat from all the bodies jammed in the kitchen had me shaking my head.

"Not in here. There's more room out in the barn. I'm sure there's something you can use out there for a table."

Fey and human alike quickly left the house. Even Molev went to watch, leaving Drav and me alone for the first time since waking here.

Drav seemed to have the same thought because he leaned

down and brushed his lips against the exposed skin of my neck. I shivered at the sensation and threaded my fingers through his hair, encouraging him. It didn't stop my mind from circling around what had just happened.

"I have to ask...they went from challenging me for eating first to acting all overprotective of me. Why?"

"Because they understand you are the key to finding more women like you. Without you, the humans will not give us a chance." He turned me in his arms. "Does that bother you?"

"Nope. Not even a little. I've gotten to know you, all of you, and see you act with more honor than most humans. Any girl would be lucky to have one of you interested in her."

"Does that mean you're lucky to have me?"

"Very lucky." I stood on my toes and pulled him down for the kiss I'd been wanting since we woke.

He hungrily pressed against me, his tongue sweeping over my bottom lip before dipping inside. He gripped my hips and pulled me flush to his length. I groaned and lifted my hand to his hair, my fingers brushing over the tips of his ears.

He growled and swept me up in his arms, breaking the kiss to bolt upstairs and close us into our room. A shiver of anticipation rippled through me as he set me on my feet and snagged the hem of my shirt, pushing the material up over my ribs. The slow drag of his fingers created a blazing trail of need. Panting, I helped pull my shirt off and backed him toward the bed.

"Ready to learn something new?" I asked, heart hammering.

"Yes."

He sat on the bed and didn't resist when I robbed him of

his shirt and pushed him onto his back. His heated gaze remained locked on mine as I placed a knee on the mattress to the right of his hip and crawled forward until I straddled his waist. I let my fingertips graze the dusting of hair just below his navel as I settled my hips to his. He grunted at the contact and experimentally arched into me as his fingers dug into my hips. A zing of pleasure arced between my legs. Part of me wanted to ditch the pants and go straight to the good stuff, but there was so much he didn't know. So much I wanted to show him.

"It gets better," I whispered, bending down to place a kiss on his throat then chest.

His fingers stroked over my skin, skimming down my spine then coming around to try to cup my breast as I slowly made my way down to his belly button. His breathing grew harsher with each press of my lips. Sliding my fingers under the waist of his pants, I guided the material down until he sprang free.

He growled but held still as I brought my mouth to the tip of him.

"Do you want me to stop," I whispered.

He growled louder. I grinned and opened my mouth, barely touching the hot, smooth skin with the tip of my tongue. The feral sound Drav emitted made my heart race. I wanted him as much as he wanted me.

The sudden pounding on our door acted like a cold bucket of water dumped over my head and sent me scurrying for my shirt. Drav roared so loudly, the windows shook.

"What are you doing in there?" Molev called. "Drav said we should not open doors when you close them, but he sounds angry."

Shaking from the adrenaline spike from almost being

44

caught, I stifled my laugh by pulling my shirt over my head. When I emerged, Drav stood before me, his pants still loose. Passion raged in his eyes.

I reached out and tied his waistband again.

"We'll pick this up again when we're alone," I said softly

"No."

"This isn't something most humans do with other people around, Drav. It's meant to be private. Like at the lake. Now isn't the best time." I planted a quick kiss on his chin before stepping back and picking up his shirt to offer him.

His disgruntled expression didn't change as I moved to open the door.

"We were just spending some alone time together," I said to Molev and the few other men standing in the hallway. "Did you want me to start the movie again?"

Molev nodded, his gaze going to Drav, then dipping lower. I flushed and quickly escaped, knowing that Drav's leather pants did very little to hide the evidence of his continued erection.

After getting the fey situated with a new movie, a pouty Drav accompanied me to the barn to search the storage for something to make for lunch.

Most of the fey stood within the open door, trying to avoid the sunlight. Those without the sunglasses Bud had produced before leaving, blinked against the tears in their eyes as they focused on the current arm wrestling match. The three human men were standing back watching, shouting encouragement as the two competing fey struggled.

More of the fey men were lined up to try. I called out a warning, reminding them they couldn't rip each other's arms off, and heard a chorus of "yes, Mya," throughout the barn.

Grinning, I walked down the aisle, looking for something the fey might enjoy eating. I kept remembering how Drav had spit the pizza out.

"How about this?" Drav pulled out a box of instant potatoes.

"That might work. Let's see if we can find some meat and gravy to go with it."

Drav and I gathered a bunch of boxes into the laundry baskets, and I added cans of anything that looked like it would make a good stew. When I looked up and caught Drav watching me hungrily, I knew we needed to head back to the house.

In the kitchen, we set the baskets on the tables.

"How can I help?" he asked.

He brushed my hair back from my face, his hand lingering on my cheek. I brought my hand up to cover his and pressed a kiss to the palm of his hand.

"You already are."

FIVE

The sun had already started to set by the time we heard shouts from the front gate. My heart kicked up a notch from where I was snuggled against Drav on the couch.

"The scouting group is back," he said.

"Come on." I stood, anxious to learn what the group had found.

Outside, the gate was just grating open for the line of fey on the road. As the men jogged into the crowded yard, I noted the clean paths on their dusty cheeks, evidence that their eyes had watered throughout the day, despite the sunglasses.

I frowned at the sight of Bud flung over the last fey's shoulder.

"What happened?" I asked over the sound of the gate closing behind them.

"What happened," Bud answered, "is that these assholes wouldn't let me set the pace."

The fey carrying Bud dropped him like an unwanted sack of potatoes. Behind me, I heard a few soft "arm wrestle" comments and almost grinned.

Bud grunted and climbed to his feet with an angry glare.

"You didn't tell me how fast they would want to run. As soon as I couldn't keep up, one of them tossed me over his shoulder without giving me a choice. I couldn't see shit that way."

"No sign of Will or Tubby?" Jerry asked.

"None," he said bitterly. Bud started off toward the barn and the rest of his men quickly followed. I looked at the nearest fey.

"Would you be willing to follow them? Keep your distance, but watch what they do and listen to what they say, if you can."

He nodded. Three of his friends went with him. Once they left, the group's mood turned from tension to open reunion as those who'd been out scouting welcomed the fey who'd joined us since they left. There had to be close to two hundred of the fey on the surface now.

"Ghua, what news?" Molev asked over the greetings.

"We passed several cities. Some whole. Some destroyed."

"Any signs of humans?"

"No. We did find a new safe place, though, north of here. It's just outside a city Bud knew. He called it Ardmore. The large building has a lot of land with a high fence around all of it. Safe enough to stay for a night or two as we scout further."

I hated the idea of more sitting and waiting just because Bud and his friends wouldn't talk. I glanced at the barn where they'd disappeared inside.

"Did you tell Bud we were looking for a new place to stay?" I asked.

"No. He thought we were looking for humans."

"What are you thinking, Mya?" Drav asked when I continued to stare at the barn.

I sighed. "I'm thinking that it would be dangerous to let those guys know we're leaving or where we're going. I wish they would just tell us if they knew something, but I understand their fear. I'm going to try talking to them again and see if Bud's attitude can be persuaded to change." I put my hand on Ghua's arm. "Thank you for scouting and putting up with Bud. I'm betting it wasn't easy."

Ghua grinned slightly. "His mouth tempted me to leave him to the infected when they trapped us inside the warehouse."

"They what?" I said, dropping my hand.

The image of the infected woman outside my window popped into my head, and a tingle of apprehension shivered over my skin.

"Let's go inside," Molev said. "The scouting party can sit and eat while Ghua tells his story."

Once inside the house, Drav and I scooped out four portions of stew and brought the bowls to the table. We sat to listen to Ghua as the rest of the men began serving themselves.

"How did you get trapped in a warehouse?" I asked.

"The first time we came up here, the stupid ones moved around as if they were lost until they heard something. Then, they ran. The second time I came up to tell everyone to leave the surface, they seemed less lost. This time, they don't seem as stupid."

"When we reached the first town, a line of cars stretched across the road and far into the trees on both sides. Bud moved toward the cars, not seeing the lone person standing in the road further away. Farco reached out to stop him. Before he did, the infected made a noise. It wasn't a word, but a long, loud groan. More infected swarmed from the woods. Only twice our number. We removed their heads while Bud cried and yelled. The infected down the road had disappeared by the time we'd finished."

"That's disturbing," I said. "More than disturbing, really, but I don't know that I would really describe that as being trapped, though."

"We were trapped in the warehouse, Mya, not the street."

The way he said it almost made me grin.

"I'm sorry. Continue."

"After that, we didn't see any infected until we reached Ardmore. Standing alone in the road was the same infected. He wore a red shirt and only had one shoe. He didn't call out this time. Instead, he turned and ran. We followed, chasing him into a warehouse. The door closed behind us. Bud was yelling because it was dark, but we could see and smell. Decay soured the air in the building from the hundreds of infected waiting within. It was good that Bud could not see all of them."

My stomach dropped at Ghua's description, and I sincerely hoped this was like a fishing story. One embellished to make the retelling more interesting.

"What did you do?" I asked, leaning forward, food long forgotten. Most of the men in the kitchen lingered to hear the end as well.

"I considered throwing Bud to them, but we climbed the metal logs supporting the ceiling and ripped open the tin roof."

"Why didn't you just rip open the door?"

"I wanted to see what the infected would do."

"And?"

"They didn't do much. They couldn't climb like we could. After the warehouse, we left the city and found the fenced-in place. The return trip was much quieter," Ghua finished.

"Eat, Mya," Drav said softly, nudging the bowl toward me.

I picked up my spoon and ate a few bites as I considered everything. Although I trusted Ghua's word, he knew very little of humans, uninfected or otherwise. Maybe what he'd thought was a sign of intelligence was just his lack of understanding. Or maybe I just didn't like the idea of smarter infected.

"I need to talk to Bud," I said, pushing the bowl aside.

"Why?" Drav asked.

"I don't like the idea of shuffling around from place to place in a blind attempt to find the safe zones. I'm hoping after a day with Ghua and the others, he might be more willing to share whatever information he knows.

"I'm also thinking about telling him we're leaving. Part of me thinks that's a bad idea. That they'll go running to whoever they'd thought had shown up when Ghua arrived. Yet, the other part of me feels...I don't know. Worried maybe? They have two men out there who haven't come back. How long will four humans last against the infected and hellhounds, even with this fence protecting them?"

"I think you should tell them," Molev said. "If they go to tell other humans, then your people will find us."

"Yeah, that worries me. You saw how they destroyed the cities. I'm worried they will try to do the same to you if we can't find and talk to them on our terms."

Molev shrugged. "I still see no reason to remain quiet. Perhaps they tell other humans, and we find women sooner. Perhaps they come with us, and we must look longer. We cannot know the outcome until we make the choice."

"All right," I said, standing. "I'll go talk to them."

Drav stood, too.

"Together," he said.

"Together," I agreed.

His company came in handy when we walked into the barn to an openly hostile one-sided argument between Bud and the four fey who'd been keeping an eye on the men.

"Is there a problem?" I asked Bud, interrupting his tirade about privacy.

"Yeah, tell them to get lost."

"They're keeping an eye on you because I asked them to," I said, walking toward the aisles of supplies.

"Why, and what are you doing?" he asked, angrily following in my wake. "Leave our supplies alone. You've taken enough."

"You're right. We have." I turned to look at the man. Drav stood inches behind him, the intensity in his gaze a bit awe-inspiring. Bud wouldn't even be able to sneeze in my direction without immediate intervention by Drav.

"We're leaving. Tomorrow morning, if I have my way."

"Good," he said with a satisfied smile.

"Is it? You said you're missing two men. How long do you think just the four of you will be able to stay here on your own?"

"Long enough."

"That's such a macho bullshit answer. The real answer is not long."

"We'll last plenty long if you give us our guns back."

I shook my head, not in denial but annoyance.

"You'll get them when we leave and not before." I glanced past him to his men who watched us and listened. "If any of you want to come with us, you'll be welcomed and protected."

I looked at Bud again. "What happened in the warehouse?"

"How the fuck would I know? Those idiots ran into a pitch-black building. I couldn't see a damn thing."

"What about what you smelled or heard?" I asked.

"I didn't smell or hear nothing."

The steady almost daring way he held my gaze told me the truth. Ghua hadn't embellished.

"Right. You weren't stuck in a building filled with infected who only wanted to rip you apart so they could taste fresh human flesh. I get that you're not worried about you. That's fine. But think of everyone else out there. You wouldn't be standing here right now if it weren't for the fey. There are other survivors out there who need their help. Please, tell me where they are."

His eyes narrowed.

"There ain't nothing to tell, demon whore," he said with menace.

Drav growled low behind him, and I had the pleasure of watching Bud pale.

"Fine. We'll see you again in the morning. Enjoy your night," I said, walking past him to Drav. Drav wrapped an arm protectively around my shoulder and led me to the others.

"Keep watch," I said. "All night. I don't trust them." I didn't bother to lower my voice.

Outside, Drav scooped me up into his arms.

"Why do they keep calling you something you are not?" he asked, pressing his forehead to mine.

"They use insults to try to make me as angry as they are. By staying calm, I'm robbing their insults of any power. Next time, ignore them. It will make you the bigger man."

"I already am the bigger man."

I grinned knowing he meant that literally.

"Let's go to bed, big guy. We have a long day ahead of us tomorrow. There's no reason to stay here if everyone who's coming from the caves has joined us. It's time to start seriously looking for my family."

No one stopped us as we made our way to the bedroom. Most of the men already lay wherever they could find an open spot. Ghua once again rested on the floor beside our bed.

Drav didn't say anything about all the bodies crammed into the room. He just set me on the bed and snuggled close. I toed off my shoes and closed my eyes.

Tomorrow, for better or worse, we would leave this place.

Six

The smell of bacon tickled my nose. I sat straight up in the mostly dark room and inhaled deeply, not believing what I smelled.

"No way."

I bolted from the bed, and like a pro hurdler, I cleared the bodies on the floor. Drav called my name as I sprinted down the steps, waking up the men along the way with my racket. The sun hadn't yet kissed the horizon so I whispered "go back to sleep" as I passed.

Rounding the corner to the kitchen, I found Jerry at the stove, guarding three pans full of the greasy meat. Molev watched from the table.

"That smells like heaven," I said, moving close to Jerry. "Where did it come from?"

"The freezer on the back porch. It's full of meat."

"Damn."

"Bud was glad you didn't notice it. But I figured if you're leaving today, you might want something that reminds you of home." He shrugged as if what he'd done was no big deal.

I studied him, noting the worry in his face. Likely for me. He knew what to expect out there. He'd been living it for weeks. And, I had no real idea, but I did know the fey would keep me safe.

"Come with us," I said softly. "You spent all day with these guys yesterday. You had to learn a little bit about them in that time. They're no better or worse than us. They have faults, but they have strengths too."

"I know. I'm not staying because I don't trust them. I'm staying because my friends need me. We've lost too many already, and I can't do that to them." He set his fork aside. "Now that you're awake, I better get back out to the barn before Bud notices. He's been arm wrestling most of the night." A slight grin followed that statement.

"Thanks for the bacon," I said, watching him as he walked away.

Drav entered the kitchen to the sound of the door closing behind Jerry.

"Good morning, Mya. Is this the food you crave?" he asked, standing behind me and wrapping his arms around my waist.

"Oh yeah. Bacon and eggs. I never thought I'd eat that again."

He watched me nudge the bacon around the pans while I waited for the salty meat to finish cooking. Once it was crisp enough, I removed all of it from the pans and set a heaping plate full on the table. Neither Drav nor Molev seemed too impressed when they tried a piece. I didn't mind. It meant more for me.

Men slowly trickled into the kitchen and tried bits of the bacon before going outside.

"We're leaving this morning, right?" I asked, looking at Molev.

"Yes. According to Ghua, we should be able to reach the building before the sun is too high."

"Good. The humans are going to stay here. We can't leave them defenseless. Where are their guns?"

"In the back of the barn next to the sacks of rice."

"In plain sight?"

"Yes."

"How did you know they wouldn't find them and try to use them?" I asked.

"Someone was always with them. They wouldn't have gotten close."

I didn't argue, but he probably saw the doubt on my face.

"I'm going to head upstairs, shower, and pack. It shouldn't take me too long to be ready."

Drav followed me upstairs.

"You should see if any of the clothes in these dressers fits you. It doesn't hurt to have something clean to change into," I said as I set my bag on the bed. While he looked through drawers, I pulled a clean set of clothes out of my bag.

He didn't say anything when I left the room.

In the bathroom, I brushed my teeth and looked at myself in the mirror. I didn't look different. Not really. But I felt so different. Older. More tired. More determined, with a clear goal. Find my family and a way for all of us to rebuild our world, together.

Turning from the mirror, I started the shower and stripped. Not wanting to waste time, I stepped into the chilly spray and began washing. Physically, I felt recovered from my time in the caverns, which was a good thing. Even though Drav would likely carry me the whole way to the new place, I would still need my strength and wits about me in the days to come. Because, while my goal might have been clear, how to achieve it still remained a mystery, especially given the reaction of the humans to the fey.

The water had just begun to warm when the door opened. I rinsed my face and stuck my head out of the curtain to catch Drav in the process of stripping.

"Uh...what are you doing?"

"Showering with you."

My gaze shifted to his erection.

"I'm not sure that's a good idea. Molev wants to reach the building before the sun gets too high. Showering together is going to slow us down."

"No, it will save time." He swept the curtain aside and stepped in with me.

My pulse jumped at the first brush of his fingers over my water slicked skin. I should have said no, but I couldn't. Not when he took the soap from me and ran his foamy hands over my shoulders in slow gentle sweeps. I closed my eyes and let him wash me, relishing the feel of skin on skin. Each soapy caress over my breasts made my breath catch. He didn't rush, and I didn't want him to. As he washed my chest, he nibbled his way from my collarbone to my jaw. I wrapped my arms around his neck and waited for his lips to meet mine.

Instead of kissing me, he coaxed me to release my hold and turn around. The spray of the shower rinsed my front as his hands slid over my shoulders and down the long line of my back. I held still as his hands swept over the curve of my ass and cupped me, but I ached for more than just a washing.

He reached around me and set the soap on the ledge.

Before I could turn to rinse again, his hands gripped my hips, and he pulled me against his chest. One hand anchored me to him while the other slid over my abdomen and down to my curls. I reached up behind me, digging my fingers into his hair.

"I love the sounds you make," he murmured in my ear as he parted me.

I tried not to make sounds. Really, I did. But when his finger brushed over my sweet spot again and again, I came apart with a pained-sounding mewl. I turned my head up to him, and he kissed me hard, capturing most of the sound.

Trembling with aftershocks, I kissed him in return until he pulled away, turned me, and placed his forehead against mine.

"I love you, Mya."

Tears welled in my eyes for the beautiful, sincere man holding me. My heart ached for what I felt for him. Was it love? I thought so. But the fear I had for our future fought so hard to stifle it.

"We better finish up, Drav, before Molev bursts in again."

Drav didn't seem to mind that I hadn't returned his sweetly worded sentiment. When I took the soap and helped him wash, I paid all his parts as much attention as he'd paid mine. Kissing him didn't keep his growls quiet, though.

His release echoed in the bathroom, and I didn't stop touching him until the last shudder wracked through him. He kissed me tenderly, and I was glad I hadn't fought showering together. Even though he'd never left my side, I'd missed him like he had left me. We'd needed this.

Someone knocked on the door.

"We are meeting in the yard," Molev said through the wood.

"Okay. We'll be just a minute," I called back.

Drav kissed me hard then turned off the water. Pushing the curtain open, Drav grabbed the waiting towel and handed it to me before getting his own.

We hurriedly dried and dressed. Well, I dressed. Drav left the bathroom without wearing a stitch of clothing. No one in the hallway seemed to even notice.

Drav put on a clean shirt and the same pants in our room while I brushed and braided my wet hair in the bathroom. We both walked downstairs a few minutes later. Most of the fey had left the house. The few remaining ate soup in the kitchen.

Stepping outside, we found the majority of the fey milling about the yard in the pre-dawn light. Molev called Drav's name, gesturing him over toward the barn where he stood with some other long-haired fey.

"Go. I'll walk around before we have to leave," I said, waving him off and shouldering my bag. He pressed a kiss to my forehead and went to join Molev.

I wandered over to the gate. I didn't think we were that far from Irving, which meant we had a lot of road to cover to get to the new place. It wouldn't take the fey long, though, at the speeds they traveled.

While the others wandered about, I watched the trees through the fence. Shadows danced among the barren trees, the branches rustling in the wind, creating creaking groans as bark scraped against bark.

The woman from the day before and Ghua's story rose to my mind again. How many infected lurked in those trees lining this road and the next?

Suddenly, I no longer felt so eager to leave.

I stepped back, ready to turn away from the fence when something in the trees caught my eye. A trace of red amidst the brown. I leaned forward, focusing on the spot. There it was again. A small figure moving through the forest. I watched the uneven way it moved, and my heart broke. As much as I wanted it to be a fox or some other creature, I knew it wasn't. A child had become infected and now wandered the woods, forever alone.

The figure stumbled from the trees into the road, tottering closer with each uneven step. Close enough that I could see its tousle of black hair. A little boy, no more than three or four years old, lifted his head. I caught a glimpse of his baby blues as he stumbled then threw his hands out to catch himself.

My hands gripped the chain link gate, and I gasped, not believing what I was seeing. Blue eyes without a trace of cloudiness. The child was not infected, just thin and dirty. How was he still alive out there?

The boy regained his feet and wobbled forward, each step a monumental struggle. I finally saw why. A heavy, thick loop of rope had been tied around his waist. The end trailed after him and disappeared into the trees from where he'd emerged.

Fear gripped me. Who had tied him?

I reached out and grabbed the fey beside me.

"Do you see the human?" I asked, not taking my eyes from the boy.

"Yes, Mya."

"Go get him. But be very gentle. There's a rope around his waist. I don't know why. Hurry and be careful."

The fey jerked the gate open and sprinted toward the boy. The child stopped walking, shocked at the sight of the big grey man coming his way. The toddler's bottom lip wobbled.

The rope behind him moved. The slack began to tighten. Something held the other end.

"Quick," I yelled. "The rope!"

The fey reached the boy and quickly untangled the rope from his tiny waist. A loud gurgle sounded beyond them.

From the trees, a herd of infected emerged, racing toward the fey and the boy. The number of infected spilling from the forest stunned me. Amidst the chaotic movement, one stood still. A woman in a torn and dirty brown business suit. The woman I'd seen outside my window. She held the other end of the rope.

Terror coursed through me as the fey lifted the child into his arms and sprinted toward the gate, barely ahead of the infected.

Across the yard, Bud started yelling, demanding their guns. I hoped the fey were smart enough not to give the humans the weapons.

"Get Mya away from the gate," Drav shouted.

Strong arms wrapped around my waist and yanked me off my feet. As I was carried away from the gate, I couldn't stop watching the scene play out.

The fey and child made it into the yard with the herd of infected right on their heels. Men tried to force the gate closed as the infected crashed against the fencing, the sound of grunts and groans filling the air along with eager yells.

I swatted at the arm holding me.

"Stop. Put me down." The fey listened, but he stayed close to my side.

"Get the kid to the house," I yelled. The man, who still

held the boy in his arms, heard me and sprinted in that direction.

The rest of the fey moved toward the fence, ready. On the other side, the infected pushed harder against the metal barrier. One fell. The infected behind him stepped on his back, reaching closer to the top.

Metal groaned. Fear clawed at me as the gate's hinge twisted under the weight of so many infected. Infected spilled into the yard. The nearby fey met them with a brute strength that sent the first infected head flying from its body.

"Protect Mya and the child," Molev's voice called out from somewhere in the fray.

The fey beside me nudged me back toward the house as infected swarmed the men nearest the gate. I couldn't tear my eyes from the fight as fey began to disappear under the swell of bodies pouring through.

Bud continued to yell for weapons. Weapons wouldn't help against these kinds of numbers. Only the fey could.

Not a single infected made it a step in the direction of the house—my direction—because of the number of fey lined up to meet them. The sickening sound of tearing flesh filled the yard. Heads began to sail through the air as the fey pressed forward, clearing infected from those in the front. Heads weren't the only thing flying. With a thunderous yell, one of the fey sent a body flying over the chaos. The limp headless infected landed outside the fence.

"In the melee, I saw an infected slip between two fighting fey and go for Bud. I opened my mouth to call out a warning at the same time Bud saw the infected. The man grabbed Butch and pushed his friend toward the creature.

The infected pounced on Butch, and Bud turned to sprint into the barn.

In horror, I watched Butch struggle with the woman. Bodies blocked my view for a moment, and the fey with me nudged me further toward the house. There were still infected pouring in through the gate, though.

"Go help them. I only need one of you. We can't afford to lose any of you. Go!"

Half the fey guarding me broke off to help their friends. I caught sight of Kerr racing toward Butch and the infected that had him pinned against the barn. He ripped the infected away from the man by grabbing the infected woman's hair and shoulder. His biceps bulged as he separated head from body. As Butch slowly slid down the barn's wall, Kerr turned back to the fight.

Within minutes, the fey eliminated the remaining threat. Bodies littered the blood-stained ground, and the fey began tossing infected parts over the fence.

I shuddered at the sight and focused on the men by the barn. Bud had reemerged, and Butch still sat on the ground, a hand pressed to his shoulder.

I strode over to them.

"What happened?" I asked. Blood seeped through Butch's fingers and shirt.

"Nothing, demon-bitch," Bud said.

"He was bit," Jerry said.

"Fucker pushed me," Butch panted, pulling his hand away to reveal the bite on his shoulder.

Gnarled, torn flesh flapped against the remaining skin and blood poured from the wound. I held in my gag and focused on

Butch's face. I didn't know what would happen to him. Every person who had turned infected that I'd witnessed since this thing started had been because a hellhound had killed them. But I knew from Charles, a bite from an infected caused the sickness to spread, too.

I squatted down in front of Butch and met his pained gaze.

"How long do you have?"

"Not long," Jerry answered for him.

I reached out to put a comforting hand on Butch's leg, but Drav stopped me with a hand on my shoulder.

"No, Mya."

I hadn't even realized he'd joined us.

"What happens now?" I asked.

"Give us the location of the guns so we can put this fucker out of his misery," Bud said.

I stood and looked Bud in the eye.

"I saw what you did. I wish I had the strength to hit you in the face and break your damn nose." No sooner had the words left my mouth than Drav's fist darted forward and made my dreams come true.

Bud howled in pain as blood poured from his nose.

Ignoring him, I squatted back down by Butch.

"Thank you for that," he said.

His breathing hitched, and he groaned in pain. Drav jerked me back, well out of the man's reach.

A moment later, Butch hunched over. He clutched his stomach and threw up. The other men jumped backwards as bile and breakfast splattered on the ground. Butch kept dry heaving.

"Butch?" Jerry stepped forward, but Tucker stopped him

65

with a hand on his shoulder.

"Don't, there isn't anything we can do."

"FFFFFuuccck," Butch moaned, straightening enough to lean back on the barn.

His eyes watered, and tears fell down his cheeks. My stomach became queasy as I noticed blood coated around his mouth. In a moment, he fell forward onto the ground. He made no noise, and the area around us became utterly silent.

"Butch?" I said.

A muffled groan came from the fallen body at our feet, and slowly Butch got back to his feet. His milky white gaze swept over us, his mouth opening and closing listlessly.

SEVEN

Drav stepped protectively in front of me and immediately removed Butch's head. Crisis averted, he tossed the head to Kerr and turned to me. For a moment, my brain couldn't process how quickly Butch had gone from a person with an attitude to a mindless abomination. There were so few of us. One bad decision, one bite, just took another. At a loss, I stared at Jerry and Tucker as a nearby fey stepped forward and removed Butch's body.

"You wanted to know what the world was like?" Bud demanded in a nasally voice. "What you missed? That is what you missed."

Something flickered in Jerry's gaze. Anger. Maybe hate. I felt the same toward Bud. Without acknowledging the asshat's comment, I addressed Jerry and Tucker.

"You're both still welcome to come with us; but if you decide to stay, watch your backs around him. He'll push you next if it means saving himself."

I turned to go to the house and stopped short at the sight of Drav and Molev standing in front of me. Blood and gore caked their hands and arms.

"You guys are a mess. Do you want to shower?"

"No. It will take too long, and we will probably need to do this again before we reach the next safe place," Molev said.

I nodded slowly and glanced at Drav.

"You're not carrying me like that."

"I'll shower."

We walked together to the house. The sight that greeted me in the kitchen made my eyes water. The fey, with a content look on his face, stood in the center of the room, holding the little boy he had saved. The boy's head rested on the big man's shoulder. One arm looped around the fey's neck, and his little hand gripped the man's braid. He sucked the thumb of his other hand, his tear-streaked face turned toward us.

His gaze kept flicking between me, Drav, and Molev.

"Go get cleaned up," I said to Drav. "The less people in here right now, the better."

Drav went upstairs, and Molev retreated outside once more. The boy sighed gustily, the exhale hitching a bit from his recent crying.

"Hi there," I said softly. "My name is Mya. What's your name?"

He stared at me for a moment before pulling his thumb from his mouth just long enough to say, "Timmy."

"I'm so glad we found you, Timmy. Because this house has a lot of food, and we need some help eating it. Would you like to help me?"

He shook his head no.

"That's okay. I'm just going to make some food, and if it looks good, you let me know."

I went to the sink and wet a clean washcloth, which I handed to the fey.

"For his face and hands if he'll let you. We need to get any infected blood off or he might turn, too."

The fey frowned and took the cloth.

Turning back to the cupboards, I searched until I found some peanut butter, jelly, and crackers. At the last second, I put the peanut butter back and just fixed a plate full of jelly crackers and set them on the table. My luck, the kid would have peanut allergies or something.

The fey still held the washcloth, and Timmy didn't look any cleaner.

"Here," I said, holding out my hand. The fey gave me the cloth.

"What's your name?"

"Byllo," he said.

"Okay. Timmy, Byllo's arms are getting tired. Can you sit in a chair for just a few minutes?"

Timmy lifted his head and looked Byllo in the eyes.

"They are not tired," the man said. "I could hold you forever."

"Not helping, Byllo. What do you say, Timmy? If you sit in the chair, you can have some of those crackers I made."

The boy looked at the table, and his eyes lit up at the sight of the crackers. He wiggled in Byllo's arms, and the man bent to set him on a chair.

"Hold on, Timmy. First, we need to wash your hands and face, right?" The boy held his hands out to me and waited patiently while I wiped them and his face.

"There's a spot on your face this washcloth isn't getting. Is it okay if Byllo lifts you up so you can wash in the sink?

"Yes."

Byllo carefully picked the boy back up and held him steady

while Timmy and I worked together to wash his hands and face with soap at the sink. By the time we finished, Timmy's stomach growled continuously.

"While you eat those, I'm going to see what we have to drink."

Based on how the boy looked, he'd been without food for a while, and I worried it would be the same for fluids. I poured a cup of water and set it in front of him.

"Byllo, can you go to the barn and see if there are any cans of evaporated milk and maybe a bag you can use to carry them? Ask Jerry. We'll need some for Timmy."

The fey left. Timmy paused his eating to stare at the door.

"Byllo will be right back," I said, sitting. "He's going to get some stuff so you won't be hungry or thirsty at the next place we stay."

The boy shifted his gaze to me, concern lighting his eyes.

"How old are you, Timmy?"

He held up four fingers.

"That's pretty old. I bet you know a lot of stuff. I know a lot, too. Have you noticed how some people are sick and not acting very nice?"

He nodded.

"My mommy, daddy, and sissy got sick."

"Aw, Timmy..." Struggling not to cry, I cleared my throat and gently smoothed my hand over his head. "I'm really sorry about your family getting sick. Byllo can't get sick. He's strong and fast and very nice. So are all his friends. After you're done eating, we're going to go look for the rest of the people who aren't sick."

"Do I have to wear a rope?"

"No. Never again." I wanted to ask him about that but doubted it would do anything more than scare him. "Would you like some peaches or pears to eat next?"

"Yes, please."

I smiled and grabbed a can of each.

Drav entered the kitchen one slice before Timmy polished off his can of pear halves.

"Drav, this is Timmy. Timmy, this is my friend Drav. He's really nice like Byllo."

"Hello, Timmy," Drav said, approaching us.

"Your eyes are funny," the boy said, staring up at Drav.

"Not funny," I said. "Just different. He can see better at night."

A look of terror crossed the boy's features when I had said night.

"It's okay, Timmy. You'll be with us now. We'll keep you safe." The words barely left my mouth when Byllo came in, followed by Bud, Tucker, and Jerry.

"Like hell you're taking the kid or the fucking supplies. Both stay with us," Bud said.

Timmy stared at him with wide eyes. Byllo set the two cases of evaporated milk on the counter and came to stand beside the boy.

"If the fact that you just pushed your friend into an infected to save your own skin isn't enough of a reason to disqualify you for child care, the fact that you swore is. Leave, Bud, before one of these guys makes you."

Bud stormed out.

"You're welcome to whatever you need," Tucker said. "We'll be pulling out right after you do. We've got a place we can go."

He didn't need to say it was a place where we wouldn't be welcome. I could see that in his eyes.

"I hope you get there safely. Tell them everything, Jerry. And be honest about it."

"I will," he promised before heading out the door.

"We need to leave, Mya," Drav said.

"I know." I looked at Timmy. The boy had a smudge of jelly on his chin. Much better than infected blood.

"You ready, sweetie?"

His nod set in motion a swift departure. Byllo carried Timmy and stayed close to Drav, who carried me. No one spoke as they sprinted out the corpse-riddled gate and down the road. All of the men remained alert as we passed the discarded rope and trees.

The sound of an engine roaring to life behind us made me cringe. After what we'd just gone through, I couldn't help but feel on edge.

Molev motioned to Ghua. Ghua nodded and, along with five others, broke off from the group and slipped into the trees. Staying true to the ingrained need to remain quiet out in the open, I said nothing.

The sun rose and some of the tension left me as miles swiftly passed under the fey's feet. It wasn't just our progress that soothed me, but little Timmy. Having him with us worried me, but it also made me feel so much less alone. I looked over at the boy as he sucked his thumb and dozed in Byllo's arms. The man kept glancing down at the kid, too. He wasn't the only one. They all did with a mix of curiosity and awe in their expressions. I couldn't imagine what it would be like to only know adults and then discover an adorable tiny version existed.

We traveled for almost an hour before Timmy woke and started fidgeting. I called a stop, helped him go to the bathroom, and gave him something to drink. Byllo was right there to pick him up again when it was time.

The boy never really made a sound. Seeing someone that age so subdued felt unnatural. What had the child gone through before we'd rescued him? Still, not a single bite marked him. That, along with the rope, could only mean one thing. The infected had known to use a healthy human as bait.

When we reached the blockade of cars outside of Ardmore, blood smeared the faded blacktopped surface. The wide path of red veered to the left into the trees.

Molev slowed the group, keeping well back from the vehicles, and silently motioned left and right. Twenty men broke off in each direction. Just as they left us, a single person stepped into view further down the road. The creature emitted a creepy as hell sound that made me want to run the other way. In seconds, grunts and groans came from the woods on either side of us. However, nothing emerged.

A creak of metal drew my attention to the line of cars. The trunk of a vehicle slowly opened. The back door of another unlatched.

"Byllo, turn Timmy away so he doesn't see this," I said softly as the first fey man stepped forward.

Molev didn't mess around with the infected crawling from the blockade. He ran forward into the line of cars, pushing the two central ones wide apart. He didn't stop there. Gaining speed, he ran for the infected leader while the remaining fey cleaned out the cars.

After hearing Ghua's story about how they'd been led into a trap, I appreciated Molev's foresight to kill the apparent infected leader immediately. He tossed the head aside and motioned for us as the fey dispatched the final infected from the cars.

The men who'd disappeared into the woods reappeared, dirtier than before. One had a bit of gore stuck to his cheek, and I hoped the new place we were headed had more than one bathroom.

It took hours to reach our final destination. Hours of moving quickly and quietly. Hours of watching the trees beside the road for signs of infected. However, other than that first group, we never saw any more up close.

All that effort seemed such a waste as I studied the building before us. Sure it had a protective fence and space enough where we could all fit and be safe during the night, like I'd specified. However, the cold distribution factory was far from the cozy farmhouse we'd left behind.

Molev led us up the drive to the gated entrance.

I glanced at Byllo, who walked nearby with Timmy draped against his shoulder. The boy's sleep relaxed face made me smile slightly. He obviously felt safe with Byllo. I just hoped the little guy wouldn't freak out when he woke and saw our new temporary home.

The clatter and groan of metal drew my attention back to the gate where Molev and a few others forced their way in.

"Wait here," he said.

He motioned for a group of ten. They moved toward the building and disappeared inside through the main doors. I felt safe enough in the open, held securely in Drav's arms, but I wasn't so sure how I'd feel inside.

The place felt creepy in its abandonment. Semi-trailers sat forgotten at docks that would never again be used. Cars remained in the parking lot for owners who would never return. Nothing moved except the dried grass that had grown up around the fenced perimeter. No sound reached my ears except the soft shuffle of the fey's feet as they kept watch.

While we waited, the sky began to cloud over. Without the sun, the temperature dropped. I shivered in Drav's arms and knew Timmy would be getting cold, too.

Not long afterward, one of the scouts returned.

"We removed a few infected. Molev says to come in," he stated.

A couple of the men stayed behind to close the gate while the rest of us entered the building. The high ceilings of the warehouse produced an echo of our footsteps as we passed the metal shelving lining the factory floor. Untouched by the chaos outside its doors, the shelves in this place still had boxes and boxes of now useless electronics.

The fey fanned out, checking out our temporary home. My eyes swept the large room again. With so much space, I worried about spreading out too thin. As we learned at the last place, a fence only provided so much protection if the infected found us.

I glanced up at the second-floor platform and saw windows with blinds. Likely an office.

"I think it's safe enough for me to walk," I said, glancing at Drav. "I want to explore upstairs."

Drav grunted, put me down, and followed me to the old office. Our footsteps echoed loudly on the sturdy metal stairways bolted to the wall.

At the top, I looked out over the vast warehouse and spotted a couple of different entrances.

"You'll want someone posted at each exit," I said, pointing them out.

Seeing the fey try to find places to sit and rest, I realized not only would there be no showering, there would be no food or comfort either. Not until we went out to find some supplies.

We had all traveled extremely light, most with only the clothes on our backs. We needed food, water, warmer clothes for Timmy, clean clothes for the men, soap, towels...the list of supplies kept getting longer. I chewed my bottom lip, knowing we would have to head into Ardmore to get supplies.

On the way here, the glimpses I caught of the town showed it free from any bomb destruction. That meant an infected infestation. Although the fey had swiftly dealt with the infected on the road, the idea of going into any area where there would be even more infected worried me. As it should, I supposed.

Turning away from the view, I opened the office door. Paperwork still covered the desk, waiting for the manager who had probably assumed he would be back the next day to finish. It felt odd to see that there were pockets of the world I'd known still untouched by devastation. Quiet little pieces suspended in time. The thought left an open wound in my heart. Our old world was gone.

Drav moved behind me, reminding me of our task.

"This wouldn't be a bad place to sleep. Some of those empty boxes from down below will keep us from getting cold on the floor. We could bring one of the chairs down for Timmy to snuggle in, too." I rolled out the comfortable looking chair from behind the desk, and Drav took it from me, lifting it easily.

"We need to get supplies. It would be good to find some sunglasses for you guys if we are going to continue traveling during the day. We need food and some lightweight basics like soap and clean socks for Timmy."

I frowned as I thought of what else we needed.

Warm hands framed my face, and Drav pressed his forehead to mine.

"We will find these things. Rest your mind."

His words helped calm my rampant thoughts. In this new world, Drav was my anchor. My reality and my safety. I wrapped my arms around him, taking a moment to soak up the comfort I found simply in his presence.

He made a satisfied sound and held me close, his hands rubbing over my back. It felt heavenly, and I didn't want to move. Part of me wanted to ignore the world and just steal as much quiet time as I wanted with Drav. But I knew better. This world didn't give the unprepared any quiet time.

I sighed and pulled away.

Any thoughts of gathering supplies fled from my mind the moment I noticed Drav's hungry gaze focused on my mouth.

EIGHT

"My Mya."

The way Drav said the words set my heart racing. He changed his hold on me, reaching under my shirt so his fingertips brushed my skin.

I shivered at the contact.

He smiled slightly and lowered his head.

"Mine," he said just before his lips touched my mouth.

He kissed me tenderly, and I basked in his attention and playfully nipped his bottom lip.

He growled against my mouth, and the kiss changed, becoming more demanding. The hot palm gripping my side trailed upward until just under the curve of my breast. His fingers traced the edge of my bra then lightly moved over the cup. He teased me, circling my breast before he deftly found my nipple. I groaned into his mouth as he toyed with it through the material. His free hand gripped my butt so he could press his hips against mine, a slow rolling grind that had me gasping for air.

Just as I gripped his shoulders to pull him closer, he withdrew his hand.

"Tell me what we need, and we will find it."

I almost told him I needed him to finish what he'd started,

but a burst of sound from below brought back reality. I exhaled slowly and wrapped my arms around his waist, holding him while letting my pulse settle. After a moment, I could focus on what we needed to do and left the office to go talk to Molev about our need for supplies. Drav carried the executive chair down the stairs.

Molev had remained in the open part of the factory, watching the fey explore the place while staying close to Byllo and Timmy, who was draped over his shoulder.

"Drav, can you break the backrest off of the chair? We can use it as a bed for Timmy."

Drav snapped the chair in half like a twig and set the large, well-padded back on the ground. Byllo put Timmy down on it. The boy curled into a small ball and continued to sleep.

I stared at the child for a moment. At four, he shouldn't need so much sleep. But, given what he'd been through, I could understand why he might want it. Still, it worried me. He needed proper care.

"I want to take a small group out and scout the surrounding area for supplies," I said quietly, stepping away from Timmy.

"I will send out twenty men."

"I need to go, too." Not that I really wanted to go. I knew there'd be infected all over the place.

"No, Mya," Drav said. Molev agreed with a nod.

"It would be better if you stayed here, Mya."

"The men have learned some English, but they won't know how to read signs or know what supplies they are looking for. I can read and know what we need."

Molev looked at Drav. I did, too.

"I'll be safe with you, right?"

Drav sighed.

"Very well."

I snagged my bag and searched until I found the snack packs of applesauce I'd tucked inside.

"Here," I said, handing the containers to Byllo. "If Timmy wakes up, have him just sip this from the container. One should be good for now, but I will leave the rest for you in case he wants more. We'll bring back some better food for him. Oh, and make sure he stays in sight at all times. Little kids can get into trouble quickly without even realizing it. They are as clueless about this world as you guys were when you first came up. Only they don't learn as fast. Be patient, kind, and gentle with him. If you think I'm fragile, children are even more so."

"We will take good care of him, Mya," Molev said. "The sun is starting its descent. You should go now."

I nodded.

Molev called out for volunteers; and, within seconds, Drav and I walked outside with our group. Although the sun still floated high in the sky with no clouds in sight, I knew daylight wouldn't last much longer. The men's eyes watered as Drav picked me up and took off south, heading back the way we'd come.

The surrounding area to the left of the highway had more abandoned and ransacked buildings, so the men moved quickly, running alongside the road.

Cars, some with doors still hanging open, littered the long stretch of blacktop. The fey kept their distance from the vehicles, which I appreciated.

The highway billboards didn't help as much as the store

signs towering far above everything.

"Drav," I said, careful not to speak too loudly. "Go that way. We need to follow that road."

The fey ran past several fast food restaurants, heading further into town. After seeing the home goods store to our left, the buildings slowly began to thin out again as if we were already heading out of town. Only the signs indicating a hospital ahead kept me from telling the fey to turn around. I couldn't help but look back, second guessing myself though.

Behind us, something moved. The steady cadence of the fey's running had attracted attention.

"Infected," I said to the fey behind Drav.

A couple of the fey separated to take care of the infected. The rest of us kept going until the buildings grew thicker again. We passed more restaurants, but I ignored them. Most would have had fresh or freezer food that had long ago spoiled if the buildings had lost power.

A pharmacy on the corner of the next intersection gave me hope.

"Which way, Mya?" Drav asked.

"Go left. We'll run that way for a little bit, and if we don't find anything promising, we can turn around."

Within another block, I saw a bright blue sign that belonged to a huge chain super-center in the distance.

"There," I said softly, pointing.

Cars waited in the parking lot. Only a few had their doors open. I scrutinized the complete stillness of the surrounding area. The well-spaced business buildings remained quiet. Where were the infected? Probably near their homes. If this area had been struck at night, like everywhere else, I doubted there would have been many people in the shopping district.

Despite the logical explanation, I still felt nervous as we made quick time to the front entrance. Broken glass covered the ground, both doors smashed by looters. I hoped we'd still be able to find what we needed.

The fey's deer hide boots crunched on the debris as they stepped inside. The opaque panels in the ceiling gave just enough light to see. Other than the glass on the floor and missing items from the nearby shelves, the store seemed normal enough. The fey were cautious, though. As a group, they paused and listened. Nothing moved or made a sound as they waited.

"Check the store," Drav said. "Shax and three others stay with me."

"If there are healthy humans in here, please don't hurt them," I added.

The rest of the fey nodded and quietly moved into the store's interior.

"Can you put me down?" I asked, looking around.

I could see the produce section to our right but doubted there'd be anything worth saving there.

"Do you think it's safe to start looking for things?

"As safe as it will be."

I nodded and started forward. Shax and Drav walked beside me with the others loosely spread around us. I explored the food aisles closest to the entrance, disheartened by the sight of so many nearly bare shelves.

A sudden commotion came from further back in the store, and I looked at Drav.

"We will keep you safe. What do you need?"

"We need bags to carry the supplies in," I said.

I made my way further down the aisles toward the center of the store. The weak light from overhead caught on three carousel displays of mostly untouched sunglasses.

"We need to grab all of these. You guys should each pick out a pair to wear now and bring the rest back for everyone else."

Drav went over to the first rack of sunglasses and pulled off a pair of reflective avatars.

"Very dashing," I said sincerely.

Drav gave me a toothy smile and slipped the glasses on. Shax grunted and pulled off a similar pair to try on.

"You can use the mirror to see what you look like," I said, pointing to the reflective triangle.

He ducked down and caught sight of his reflection. He grinned and moved aside so the rest of the guys with us could try some on, too. The men who'd checked the back of the store joined us before we moved on.

"We removed a few infected. The rest of the store is quiet," one of the men said.

Drav nodded, and I watched with growing humor as the newcomers tried on several pairs of sunglasses each, checking their reflections often.

Knowing our limited time, I turned away from the fun and started toward the other side of the store.

"Where are you going?" Drav asked.

"While you guys do that, I'm going to grab some other necessities."

"Necessities? What do you need?" He removed his glasses, ready to retrieve whatever items I might require. The

83

driven way he wanted to take care of me made me feel cherished beyond belief. It also made him even more adorable in my eyes.

"You know...socks, undies, tampons. Things that will probably save my life someday," I said, unable to resist a little teasing.

His expression of idle curiosity changed to one of complete seriousness.

"I'll help you find these tampons." He strode forward with a determined gait while I trailed behind him.

"Will you carry my tampons for me?" I asked with barely contained amusement.

"I will not let them out of my sight."

I didn't have the heart to tell him they wouldn't actually save my life.

Drav and I navigated through the untouched greeting card section to the slightly raided health and beauty area. The mangled mess of what remained of the pharmacy shelves gave me little hope we would find much in the section. However, the items available surprised me. I found children's pain reliever, vitamins, and toothbrushes. Near the pharmacy, I also found some reusable shopping bags. While Drav held one, I stocked up on the things I thought we'd need. Soaps, shampoos, conditioners, toothpaste, razors, and tampons.

"This is good," I said. "Go ahead and set that by the front doors, and I'll check out the clothes."

"No. We stay together."

"They checked the store."

He continued to give me a "not happening" stare.

"Fine, but we need to hurry. I want to be safely in our

84

building by dark." I started walking toward the front doors with Drav following closely behind.

"What are some of the names of the fey who came with us?" I asked.

"Tihr, Bauts, Gyirk..."

"Okay, how good is your hearing?"

"They will be able to hear you if you need them."

"Tihr, Bauts, Gyirk, Kerr, and Shax, could you guys join us when you are done?" I couldn't help but raise my voice a little. Almost as soon as I finished speaking, the men joined us.

"Yes, Mya?" Shax said.

"Can one of you find us a couple more bags like these?" I lifted my bag holding my spoils. "Or better yet, find some duffle bags or backpacks. Something you guys can carry on your backs as we travel."

They nodded and took off. Drav and I set the first two bags by the doors then walked further into the store. I found the toys and stopped short. The shelves remained fully stocked. Of course they would be. Who would think of toys with infected and hellhounds running around? Me. I couldn't help but recall the sad look in Timmy's eyes as he lay his head on Byllo's shoulder.

"Can you go just a few more aisles down and look for blankets?" I asked Drav. "I just want to grab a few things for Timmy."

"No, Mya. We stay together."

Shaking my head at his protectiveness, I started down the aisle.

I ignored all the toys that made noise or lit up and found a box of eight crayons, a coloring book, and a small stuffed animal. It wasn't much, but for a boy who had nothing, it might just mean the world.

Turning, I handed everything over to Drav then paused to look at a brightly colored ball. Timmy would probably like it. But runaway balls led kids into streets with cars, or in this case, with infected. It would also make noise when bounced. Our new world sucked.

With one last regretful look, I moved away from the ball and led Drav to the bedding.

I loaded up his arms, and my own, with any non-bulky blankets I could find. Hopefully, the guys had located some decent bags to carry everything because the further north we traveled, the colder it would get.

Thinking of that, I moved off toward the clothing section. We crossed paths with the men. Each carried some kind of bag.

"Those are perfect," I said. "Can you go back to the food section and load up on whatever is left in cans?"

"Yes, Mya," Shax said.

"Would two of you be willing to run this stuff to the front of the store?" I hefted what I held, and two of the fey jumped forward to relieve me of my burden. They took the blankets stacked in Drav's arms, too.

"Thanks, guys. Just a few more things then we're done."

As they ran off to gather the food, Drav and I veered toward clothing.

"Timmy needs everything," I said. "He said he's four. I'm no expert on kids, but he seemed kinda small to me for that age. So I have no idea if that's actually right or not. To be safe, let's get clothing that says 5T." I showed Drav the marking on the hanger as I spoke. "He can always grow into them and have room to layer to stay warm." I held up a shirt and studied it for a moment. "Yeah, I think this will work."

"Grab five shirts and three pair of pants," I said, moving away.

"Mya," Drav said with low warning.

"I know, I know. Stay together. I'm not going anywhere. Just looking at jackets."

I found a jacket, then socks, and cute little superhero underwear. Before I knew it, I had drifted further away to grab an armful of bras for myself from the women's department. Drav stood in the men's department, stocking up on the large shirts there. I was glad he'd thought of that. Most of the men were messy from the infected run in on the road. A clean change of clothes—

Something moved quickly across the floor toward my foot. My first thought was a rat, and I jumped a little before focusing on the red toy ball.

Frowning, I bent down and picked it up. The cold wetness coating the toy surprised me, and I jerked my hand back. I turned my wrist to look at my palm. Blood covered my hand.

NINE

Heart hammering, I straightened, searching for Drav. The semi-milky, pale gaze of an infected met mine over the top of the clothing rack. It lifted a hand to its mouth and began chewing on its pointer finger. The way it tilted its head to study me, like a cat toying with a mouse, sent a shaft of terror through me.

Where the hell had it come from?

Something moved to my right. From the corner of my eye, I saw another one stand from where it had crawled between the displays of clothing. Stalking me.

With a desperate yell, I gripped the rack between us and rammed it forward to knock the first infected onto its back. Not stopping the momentum, I swung the rack around to the side. The second infected caught it in his hand and pushed back. I stumbled.

Drav yelled my name. The infected on the other side of the rack tilted its head at the sound, though its gaze never left me. It shoved the rack back at me, and I turned and sprinted in the other direction.

Drav roared behind me. As I dodged around clothing racks, I thought of Drav's stubborn insistence we stay close. I should have listened. My lungs burned from my ragged breaths.

Everything blurred in my panic, and I ran almost blindly, not sure where to go.

Turning the corner to an aisle of cookware, I skidded to a halt. An infected stood swaying from side to side on the other end. When it spotted me, it gave a low, moaning yell and raced toward me. Spinning around, I took off in yet another direction.

Drav yelled my name again.

"I'm here," I screamed.

I shouldn't have. Several moans came from different areas of the store. They were hunting us. Not us. Me. They'd seen me look at the ball and thought to use it as bait, just like they'd done with Timmy. The infected were getting far too smart.

I continued to run, the sounds of my feet giving away my location, but I couldn't stop.

Something stepped out in front of me, and I collided with it. Arms immediately closed around me, and I struggled to get free.

"Shh..."

I looked up into Shax's eyes and almost passed out in relief. Movement from the top shelf, just behind him, caught my attention. An infected, previously laying perfectly still, rolled off the shelf and onto Shax, who pushed me out of the way. I stumbled backwards. A moment later, arms closed around me again, steadying me.

Exhaling shakily, I relaxed as Shax gripped the infected's head before it could bite him.

The fetid stink of rotting flesh hit me a half a second before a low moan echoed in my ear. Horror filled me as I realized my mistake. I thrashed in the infected's hold. It didn't help. It was too late.

Teeth bit into my left shoulder, and I screamed.

The pain and fear of what would come made me crazy. Reaching back, I gripped the infected's head and bent forward with a heave. The creature flipped over my shoulder, his bite dislodging with the move.

I grunted against the pain but stayed on my feet.

Shax caught the infected and, in a blink, the creature lost its head. Not that it mattered. It had already gotten what it wanted. A taste of human flesh. The luck that had kept me alive until now had finally run out.

Shax looked up at me. His gaze immediately went to my shoulder. Before I could say anything, Drav came running around the corner, followed by three other fey. Red bathed their hands and arms.

Drav took one look at the infected laying on the ground and started giving orders.

"Search the store again." The three fey took off running.

Shax stayed, watching me with sad, guilty eyes. My stomach clenched, and fear made it hard to breathe.

Drav strode toward me, gripped my arms and leaned his forehead against mine.

"Mya," he said, ignorant relief echoing in that one word.

"I'm sorry," I said, tears welling. "I should have listened. I should have stayed right by you." A sob choked my last word.

"Shh..." he said, wrapping his arms around me. "It's okay."

My heart broke, and I shook my head slowly.

"It's not, Drav. One bit me."

He jerked in my arms and pulled back to look at me. His gaze swept over my face then settled on my left shoulder. Fear and panic spread over his features.

"Tell me what to do," he said.

I reached up and placed my hand on his cheek. Regret made my tears fall faster.

"You saw Butch. You saw what happened. There's nothing you can do but listen." I gripped his face between my hands. "You have a child with you, now. You need to protect him. You need to find my family. You need to help the humans destroy the hellhounds and clean up the infected. You can do all that. I know you can."

"Not without you," he said, leaning his forehead against mine once more. "You are the best thing here. Without you, the surface can go to hell."

"It already has. You need to save it, Drav. Please. For me."

A sudden wave of pain speared my stomach, I groaned and wrapped an arm around my middle.

"Children need a lot of care," I said, panting. "Timmy's meat has to be cooked. If you feed him raw meat, he'll get sick. Don't touch him when you're coated with infected blood, and wash his hands often with soap because he sucks his thumb."

The pain grew so intense that my knees gave out. Drav eased us to the floor and held me in his lap, tucking my head under his chin and smoothing back my hair.

"I don't know how Timmy didn't get infected already, but I want to spare him this," I said clutching Drav's shirt.

He rocked me gently, making small sounds of comfort. Exhaling shakily, I closed my eyes and tried to memorize the feel of his arms, the smell of him. We'd been through so much together. I didn't want to leave him. I wanted us to see this through to the end. Not just our journey to find my parents, but the journey of us.

Something wet dripped onto my forehead. His tears spurred my own grief.

Opening my eyes, I caught Shax's gaze. He stood back, quietly watching us, sorrow and guilt pulling at his features. I hated that I was about to add to both.

"Shax, when it's time, send Drav away and take my head. I don't want him to have to do that."

Drav growled and held me tighter, making me cry out in pain. He immediately loosened his hold and pressed a kiss to my brow, right where his tear had landed.

"No, Mya. There is a way. You said things can save you. Tell me what to do."

"Drav, there's nothing."

My insides twisted, knifing a new level of agony through me. I cried out and turned my head just in time to empty the contents of my stomach onto the cold tile floor beside us.

"No," Drav yelled, the sound echoing with each of my gagging heaves.

He held me, soothing a hand down my back again and again until I finished, then gently settled me against his chest. His ragged breathing tore at me. He knew as well as I did that the end hovered just in sight now.

I set my hand on his chest over his heart and struggled for a few beats to catch my breath. My eyes burned, but not from tears. It felt like a million needles jabbing into them. As much as I feared what was happening to me, I feared what would happen to Drav once I left.

"You're the best thing that has ever happened to me," I

said. "You terrified me at first. Then shocked the hell out of me with all your boob grabbing and pussy talk. I hate the word pussy, by the way." I pulled back and looked up at him.

The moisture in his eyes added another ache to my chest, and my effort to smile proved futile. It hurt too much. Physically and emotionally. Instead, my gaze held his.

"And, I love you, too, Drav. More than I would have ever thought possible."

He made a pained sound and brought his mouth to mine. His lips brushed mine tenderly, pouring so much into the contact it could no longer be simply defined as a kiss. It was our bittersweet goodbye to a happily ever after...to a future together, good or bad. It was a last memory he would hold onto as he walked away.

When it ended, my whole body shook.

"I'm sorry, Drav. We should have had a lifetime together." I lifted my hands and touched his cheek gently.

"You're breaking my heart, Mya," he whispered. "Do not leave me."

I closed my eyes, unable to stand the pain any longer.

DRAV…

Mya's pale skin grew paler. The blood seeping from her bite slowed as did her shaking.

"Mya, open your eyes," I said, brushing my lips over each eyelid.

She didn't do as I asked. Her exhale tickled my chin. I pressed my lips to hers again. She didn't respond. It took a moment to understand she no longer breathed. That her heart no longer beat.

Pain greater than any cursed hound bite ripped through me.

"Mya! Do not leave me!"

"Drav," Shax said quietly, "she has already left." He set a hand on my shoulder, a show of sharing in my pain. But I shrugged it off and rocked her, desperately breathing in the scent of her hair and memorizing the soft feel of her body against mine.

"You should go now," Shax said again. "I will do as Mya asked."

"No. I will see her open her eyes again."

"You would let her become what she feared? You would dishonor her wishes?"

Not all of them. Every infected and hound on the surface would die by my hands. But I would never stop protecting Mya.

I wrapped my arms around her, holding her tightly as I tipped my head back and let the world know my grief.

The building rattled with the thunderous echo of my cry.

MYA...

A heavy pain gripped my chest then eased enough that I felt the unsteady beat of my heart. I inhaled, needing air. The ringing in my ears suddenly stopped.

"She breathed, Drav. Leave, now." Shax's worried voice penetrated my confused awareness, and I struggled to open my eyes.

"You will not touch her," Drav said, anger lacing his words.

I tried to lift a hand to reassure him, but it was too heavy. My pulse thumped in my ears twice before the memory of the last few minutes clicked into place. An infected bite. My shoulder.

I gasped and forced my eyes open. Drav stared down at me, the vertical slit of his pupils wide in his grief.

"How did I ever think your eyes anything but beautiful?" I asked, my voice a rough rasp.

"Mya? You are not dead or infected," he said, raining kisses over my face.

I frowned and focused on how I felt. The pain twisting my insides didn't seem quite as bad as before.

"I don't understand. How long was I sleeping?" I asked.

Shax moved toward us.

"You were not sleeping, Mya. You were dead. Why are your eyes not white? Why are you still smart?"

"Quiet, Shax," Drav said. He demanded my attention by planting his face right in my line of sight. "Mya is smart and beautiful and alive. That is all that matters."

He kissed me hard and pulled away to stare at me again as if not quite believing it. I felt the same way.

"How? How am I still alive?" I pulled away from Drav's hold and gingerly felt my shoulder. It hurt like a bitch.

"Does it matter how?" Drav asked.

"It might. I don't know. Can you find me a mirror, Shax?" I asked.

The man ran off and returned a few moments later with part of the sunglass display. I hadn't realized we were that close to the front of the store. I took the mirror and angled it to get a look at the bite through my shirt. The infected's top row of teeth had created a deep crescent-shaped puncture but the bottom row had only left a darkening bruise on the already grey patch of skin. My mouth dropped open as a possibility came to mind.

"What happens when the infected bite you?" I asked Drav.

"Nothing," he said.

"Nothing because you had adapted with the crystal's help. Because your world is all part of the curse that created the infected. The crystal was changing me. That change was killing me, but it might have also saved me."

I had no other explanation than the time in his world had made me immune to an infected's bite.

The rest of the fey joined us and looked down at Drav and me with curious, confused expressions.

"The infected have been cleared," Kerr said. "We found a few hiding on the tall shelves."

I looked up at the shelf, remembering how the infected had hidden there and noticed the fading light.

"Drav, we need to get moving. We can't be out at dark. I'm not ready to try surviving more bites."

He stood with me in a fluid move.

"What does she mean? More bites?" Kerr asked, his gaze landing on my bloody shoulder.

"She was bitten and survived," Drav answered. "Stay close. I will not risk Mya again."

He strode toward the front of the store.

"Wait. Before we leave, I should clean and bandage the bite," I said. "All the supplies I need are back where we found the toothbrushes."

"We have the supplies you already gathered. It's not safe here."

I didn't point out that I hadn't grabbed peroxide or bandages.

"Drav, it's a risk to wait. I might have avoided turning into an infected, but there's a possibility I could still get sick in other ways."

Drav immediately veered in the correct direction.

When we stood in the pharmacy area, he set me on my feet and helped remove my shirt. I didn't care that they all watched us. Modesty went out the window after kissing death. Plus, I felt a lot safer with all of them nearby.

Shax grabbed the bottle of peroxide that I pointed out, and Drav held me as I doused the bite with the cool liquid. I gritted my teeth against the sting and kept pouring until I'd rinsed all the blood from my skin.

"Kerr, can you grab as many of those bottles as we can fit?" I said. "And all the bandages. Maybe some of those cleansing wipes, too."

The first-aid supplies were barely touched by the looters, which made sense. They'd likely passed them by for the same reason I had. Anyone hurt wouldn't likely need first aid after fifteen minutes. Anyone except for me.

While I added salve and gauze, Kerr handed Drav some of the wipes. Drav quickly cleaned his face and hands, removing any trace of infected blood.

Once I had gauze taped over the bite, I looked down at the dirty shirt we'd removed.

"Here is a clean one, Mya." Kerr held out a man's pink, long-sleeved t-shirt that had #survivor on the front.

I snorted a laugh.

"That's perfect. Thanks, Kerr."

Drav helped me ease it over my head. Although my shoulder ached, it didn't burn with pain like it had before I'd closed my eyes. In fact, other than the awful taste in my mouth, I didn't feel like a recently bitten person.

As soon as Drav tugged the shirt into place, he pressed a kiss to my forehead and lifted me gently. He started toward the entrance, but I stopped him when I spotted the pre-pasted travel toothbrushes on the aisles end cap.

"Shax, can you grab all of those and hand me one?" I said, pointing.

He tossed me a pack and loaded the rest into a bag.

While I scrubbed the taste of death from my mouth, Drav strode toward the entrance. The men picked up the supplies we'd gathered and followed us out the door.

TEN

The shock of being bitten settled over me as Drav ran. Although I breathed and thought normally, I struggled to believe I'd actually survived. That one moment...that single, stupid mistake of not seeing who had held me had almost robbed me of everything. Life. A chance to see my family again. A chance to show Drav what family meant and why they were so important to me.

I looked up at him, realizing it wasn't just my family who held that level of importance in my life now. When I lay dying in Drav's arms, I'd worried about him, too. Without me consciously realizing it, he'd made a place for himself in my life. He was my family now, too. And, he needed to know that.

He caught me looking at him.

"Are you in pain?" he asked, running faster.

I ducked my head into his shoulder to hide from the wind.

"No. The bite feels tender but doesn't really hurt." I pressed a kiss to his collarbone to reassure him. It didn't seem to work, though, because he didn't slow his pace.

With the rest of our party forming a protective circle around us, Drav ran tirelessly. The distribution factory came into sight, and I exhaled with relief seeing the fence just as we'd left it. I didn't like these new, smarter infected.

The men on guard opened the gate for us. One of the men from our group stopped to talk to the lookouts, likely to warn them about what the infected had done. Drav and the rest of the group continued their jog until we reached the main area inside the building.

"Welcome back," Molev said when Drav stopped.

While the rest of our group began emptying the bags out on the floor, Drav continued to hold me close. I didn't mind. I wasn't quite ready to let him go, either.

Resting my head on Drav's shoulder, I watched Shax sort the things we'd collected, and I studied the slow-growing piles with a sinking stomach. There hadn't been a lot of cans or dried goods left on the shelves I'd seen, but I'd hoped they'd found more while Drav and I had been collecting clothing. Seeing the cans now, though, compared to all the men who lounged around the factory floor, I knew we'd only managed to gather a small amount of food.

"You brought back more supplies than I thought you would," Molev said, studying the piles with me.

"Less than I'd hoped. We'll need more. But, we only hit one place."

Drav growled, and his hold on me tightened. Molev's gaze shifted between the two of us.

"What happened while you were collecting supplies?" he asked.

"Found a supercenter. Found some infected. Same old, same old," I said. My flippant response didn't fool Molev or calm down Drav.

"Some infected had set another trap, waiting out of sight on shelves. One bit Mya."

Molev looked at me.

"Show me," he said.

I pulled the neckline away to reveal the gauze.

"I already disinfected it and shouldn't remove the bandage until I'm ready to clean it again."

"It broke your skin, though?"

"Yeah."

"Her heart stopped beating," Shax said. "She stopped breathing."

A tremble ran through Drav's arms, and a low rumble began in his chest.

"If it's all right with you guys, I think I'm ready to lay down for a bit." I looked up at Drav and gently set a hand on his jaw. The contact warmed my chilled hand.

"I'm okay," I said softly. "Really."

Drav's gaze held mine for a moment, then he leaned down and kissed me tenderly.

I'd completely forgotten our audience until he tore his gaze from mine to look at Molev. Flushing, I focused on him, too. Molev smiled, flashing his fangs.

"Go rest. I'll tell the others to leave you alone."

Kerr handed me one of the wrapped quilts as Drav turned.

"Thank you."

Kerr nodded.

The blanket almost slipped from my arms as Drav took the stairs to the office two at a time. His rush to get me alone worried me. I'd seen Drav angry enough to not want to be on the receiving end of it. Now, he had plenty to be angry about. He'd told me repeatedly to stay close, and I hadn't listened.

"You can put me down," I said when we arrived at the top

of the stairs.

Instead of listening, he stepped inside the office with me still in his arms. The door ominously clicked shut behind us. My stomach churned, and I struggled not to let my guilt or worry show.

"Seriously, Drav. I can't make our bed if you're holding me."

He finally set me on my feet, but he didn't release me. I peeked up at him, ready to apologize again. Instead of anger in his gaze, I saw desperation and fear. He gripped my sides and pulled me close. I could feel the tremble in his hands as he set his forehead to mine.

"I can't lose you, Mya." The anguished rumble of his voice almost broke me.

How many times had he told me I was the best thing here? He'd proven time and again that I was his world. My death would have destroyed him. The thought of it still tortured him.

"You won't, Drav. Their bites won't turn me. I'm safe."

My words didn't change his grip or his shaking. He was in a dangerous place, and I wasn't sure how to help him move past what had almost happened.

I lifted my hands to his face, cupping his cheeks.

"I'm here, Drav. In your arms." I tipped my head up and gently kissed his lips. "I'm not going anywhere." I kissed him again, trying to prove my words.

His hold loosened, and his lips moved under mine. My heart leapt as I understood what he needed. I pulled back and met his tormented gaze.

Any hint of lingering doubt left me. Simply loving Drav wasn't enough. I needed to show him that he'd become my world, too.

"You're my family now, Drav. And, I'm yours."

"Mine," he echoed.

His lips crashed upon mine, demanding proof that I meant what I'd said. I gave it willingly.

When we finally broke apart, we both panted for air.

"Just a minute," I said, escaping his hold.

I moved to the windows and pulled the cord to release the blinds then went to the door and did the same. When I turned, Drav still watched me with the same desperate intensity.

"Mya..."

I walked to him, framed his face with my hands, and brought his lips to mine for another searing kiss.

"I love you, Drav," I whispered against his lips. "No matter what the future brings, I love you."

He growled low, but I knew it was his fear of losing me, not my words.

I walked away from him once more to spread the quilt out on the floor. Kicking off my shoes, I sat down on the unforgiving, makeshift bed. Drav still hadn't moved from his spot. The panicked glint still darkened his eyes, and his hands still trembled. He needed me as much as I needed him.

"Can I use you as a pillow?" I asked, holding out a hand.

As he knelt beside me, I got to my knees and wrapped my arms around his neck. I leaned in and pressed a small kiss right below his ear.

"Do you trust me?" I whispered.

"Yes."

"Then, love me back."

Drav growled and gripped my hips.

"Mya."

I couldn't help the smile that spread across my lips at the heated warning.

"Trust me," I whispered before kissing my way to his mouth.

I nipped his bottom lip. He groaned and gripped the back of my head with one hand. When his tongue traced the seam of my lips, I opened with a throaty moan. His kiss demanded everything and left nothing untouched. It started a need that grew too consuming to ignore.

Breaking the kiss, I ran my hand down his cheek, drawing my fingers over his neck until I reached his shirt.

"Your shirt needs to go," I said.

Gathering the material in my hands, I tugged it upwards. He helped, snatching the end and pulling it over his head in a quick movement.

His gaze held mine as he reached out, his fingers sweeping under my shirt and brushing over my stomach to leave trails of fire in their wake.

"Yours, too."

I reached for the bottom of my shirt, but Drav stopped me from removing it; instead, he carefully eased the material up, showing extra concern for my bandaged shoulder.

My heart melted as he removed my shirt then slipped off my bra. Bared from the waist up and still on my knees, I held still as he looked at me. Heat and hunger like I'd never seen before filled his gaze.

He reached out and reverently covered one breast with his big hand. I closed my eyes, reveling in the feel of his gentle caress. The warm, firm squeeze he gave made me ache for more. His lips settled on mine as he explored with his hands. The combination of his kiss and rough texture of his fingers heightened the sensation of each touch. I moaned as his fingers found my nipple, and gently plucked at the sensitive peak.

Slowly, he lowered us to the blanket. His lips left mine to graze kisses in a searing trail down my throat. My breath caught at the touch of his tongue to the skin over my collarbone. An ache started in my breast. His fingers, his hands, were no longer enough.

I reached up and threaded my fingers through his hair. His lips skimmed lower. I held my breath, waiting.

A second later, his mouth latched onto my tight nipple. I moaned and arched into his touch, desperate for more.

He sucked and played with the aching peak until I felt each tug in my very core. Releasing my nipple with a lick, he focused on its twin. My hands clenched in his thick hair as his mouth closed over the tip. His tongue flicked, circled, and teased, and he gave a low rumble of approval as he paid the other breast the same attention as the first.

The heat of his touch consumed me and spread lower. I slipped my hand from his hair down his back, exploring the muscled planes until I touched the waist of his pants. He growled, the vibrations doing things to my nipple and making the ache between my legs grow.

He gently pushed my hand away.

"Drav." I arched my hips, needing him to understand.

A moment later, his fingers plucked at my jeans, freeing the button and easing down the zipper. His mouth left my skin, and my heart thumped heavily in my chest as he reverently slid the material free.

Tossing my clothes aside, Drav sat back and looked at me. I swallowed hard and parted my legs slightly. Desire darkened his eyes to a forest green.

"Mine," he growled.

He stood and removed his pants. The thick erection twitched as I stared. He knelt beside me, his fingers and gaze sliding up my legs. When he reached the V, he stopped and braced a hand on each side of me. With care, he settled his weight over me. A breathy sigh escaped as his hips touched mine.

He kissed my chin and reached between us, his thumb brushing my curls and parting my folds.

"Drav..." It came out as a plea as I opened for him. His exploring fingers found my sweet spot and circled the tender flesh slowly. Bliss shuddered through me.

"I trust you, too, Drav," I said, setting my hands on his back.

He hissed out a breath, his fingers delving deeper and parting me. A moment later, he positioned himself at my entrance. His gaze remained locked on mine as he slowly pushed forward.

Each minute thrust kindled the desire growing inside me. Once he filled me, he stopped moving. I ground my hips against his, eager for more.

"You're going to need to move, or I'm going to do it for you," I said.

He grinned wickedly, his fangs dimpling his bottom lip. Then, he moved. The first stroke of his withdrawal left me breathless. The next thrust made my eyes roll closed. He set a slow, steady rhythm, and I moaned unable to keep my satisfaction to myself.

Drav rumbled his approval and moved faster. The friction sent waves of pleasure through me, pushing me toward the place where I knew even more waited. I panted and wrapped my legs around his waist. Tension coiled inside of me, building to a breaking point. I hovered there, grasping for the release that waited just over the edge.

Drav slid a hand under my hip, changing the angle of his thrusts. The hot, hard length rubbed the top of my channel, and the tension exploded in a release of pleasure, ripping a scream from me. As I arched in ecstasy, his mouth latched onto my nipple. The suction of his mouth sent another wave of pleasure through me, my walls clenching around his engorged length.

He released me and thrust deep with a roar that I was certain the remaining fey back in Ernisi heard.

Drav kissed me hard then slowly withdrew. He didn't collapse on top of me but turned us so we lay on our sides, facing each other.

"I love you, my Mya."

I brushed a kiss to his chest.

"I love you, too."

The exhaustion of the day, and being cradled in Drav's embrace had me fighting to keep my eyes open.

*   *   *   *

Still undressed, I stirred from sleep, my skin covered in goosebumps. I curled closer to Drav, seeking his warmth.

His hold tightened around me, and he pressed his lips against my forehead.

"I'll go get another blanket and some food, now that you are awake."

"No, I'm okay."

I reached for the edge of the quilt we laid on and pulled it over my exposed back.

"Your stomach has been very loud in its demand for food," he said softly, his fingers finding their way to the skin covering the insistent organ. It growled loudly again.

"Fine, but you're going to have to hurry because you're the only thing keeping me warm."

Drav sat up and tucked the blanket around me.

"I'll return quickly," he said.

Completely nude, he strode out the door.

I shook my head and fought not to blush. Hopefully, there wouldn't be too many fey awake. Sitting up, I wrapped my arms around my knees and placed my cheek against them. I sighed contentedly and reflected on what we'd done. I didn't regret it. Not a single moment. Although I still wanted to find my family, Drav was my world now. My future. There would be no going back.

Drav returned a moment later with a blanket and two cans of food. I lifted a corner of the blanket and he joined me, covering us both with the new blanket as well.

We shared the food, even though I tried to push the tuna away. Our meal didn't last long before our hunger turned into a different kind.

* * * *

As soon as the sun rose, we dressed and left the office. If the men had heard us, they didn't mention anything when we joined them on the main floor. Probably because they were too focused on the new arrivals who still slept on the cardboard piles near the shelves.

"When did Ghua get back?" I asked Molev softly.

"Not long before the sun brightened the sky." He picked up a can. "Will Timmy eat this?"

I looked at the can of fruit and nodded.

"We need to make sure we feed him a balance of foods. That's a fruit. It's good for him. But he also needs some kind of protein, like meat, beans, cheese, or milk." I picked up one of the cans of evaporated milk. "He should have one of these a day, for sure. Oh, and he needs to brush his teeth. Twice a day. You all should, now that you don't have your leaves to chew on." I caught myself before I let the conversation distract me from the question I should have asked when we'd first arrived.

"Where did Ghua go?"

Molev gave me a slight smile.

"He and a few others followed the humans when they left."

Excitement filled me. Why hadn't I thought to suggest that?

"And?" I asked.

"They stopped at a place further north and east from here. There were more healthy humans at this place."

Relief coursed through me. Now we wouldn't be wandering around aimlessly in search of a safe zone.

"That's great. Did Ghua say how long it would take for us to get there?"

"He thought we should reach the next human place just after the sun is at its highest."

"How long does he need to sleep?"

"They can wake now," Molev said.

"No, that's fine. Let them sleep. We need to divide up the supplies we brought back and repack and do a few other things before we're ready."

He let me take charge of that. I handed out the regular toothbrushes we'd grabbed, explained how to use them with toothpaste, and pointed to the employee bathrooms. Little Timmy scampered after Byllo, who also carried a child's toothbrush for the boy.

Drav stayed beside me, tracing lingering touches down my arms or over my shoulders as I inspected our final haul from the superstore. We distributed the items so if we lost a bag we wouldn't lose all of one thing. It also helped keep the bags evenly weighted, even though Drav assured me that wouldn't be an issue.

As soon as the men finished brushing, I ducked into the bathroom to clean myself up as best as I could and to check the bite on my shoulder. The whole thing had already scabbed over but remained tender to the touch.

I stared at the wound unable to believe I was still me and not some mindless infected. I thought of Drav and what would have happened to him and my family if things had gone differently. Nothing good rose to mind. Thankfully, I'd survived. Something I seemed to be pretty good at. Something I resolved to stay good at. I had a lot to live for.

Thoughts of the previous night filled my head again, and I let go of my shirt to study myself in the mirror. I still had no regrets. My family would accept Drav because I did. The rest of humanity worried me, though. The dark fey deserved to be welcomed, not shunned or subjected to suspicion. Yet, that was what they were likely to encounter. I couldn't help but wonder what else we would need to confront at the new place.

Nervously, I smoothed back my hair and re-secured my ponytail.

I wouldn't let the fey be so easily dismissed. Not this time.

ELEVEN

The safe zone didn't look like much, just a cluster of metal buildings in a large parking lot surrounded by a fence on steroids. Different forms of temporary housing had been set up near the perimeter. A few military-style tents rustled in the wind, and a weird little weather vane on top of one of the RVs shifted direction and let out a low creak. Nothing else moved. At least, not that Drav could see or hear from our current distance.

The majority of the fey waited behind the barn that belonged to the house across the road from the safe zone, a good half a mile away, while Drav watched and listened and described everything to me from a small group of trees much closer to the base.

Since arriving, Drav hadn't seen any human movement. However, Ghua assured us that Tucker and Jerry had driven right up to the gate, and it had opened for them.

Drav picked me up and sprinted back to the barn followed by the few fey who'd accompanied us close on his heels. Molev listened to Drav's description of the place.

"Do you think the humans are still there?" Molev asked me.

"Yes. I think they're just hiding. I want you guys to stay

here," I said. "Just Drav and I will go forward. When they see us, they'll come out." Probably heavily armed, but I didn't say that. "Drav, you'll need to walk behind me."

"No, Mya," Drav said, gently cupping my shoulder because of the bite. "Your body is not meant to protect me. Mine is meant to protect you."

I sighed.

"Would you listen if I said I'd rather you not come with me at all?" I asked.

"No. I won't. We will walk to the gate together."

"And we will follow at a distance," Molev said. "Not all humans are like you, Mya."

Molev and the fey hung back by the trees midway between the house and the fence while Drav and I approached the gate.

"Stop there!" a voice yelled when we stood within twenty feet.

"My name is Mya," I called. "This is Drav. We're looking for the safe zone where people from Oklahoma City would have been taken. I'm trying to find my parents."

"We know who you are," the voice called back. "You need to leave."

"Leave? Are you kidding me? Do you know what I've gone through to get here?" I took a step toward the fence, but Drav scooped me up in his arms and turned his back to the gate.

"You put me down right now, Drav," I said. The anger in my tone wasn't meant for him, but the asshole yelling at me.

"He has a gun pointed at you," Drav said.

"Leaving isn't an option. Please, Drav."

He scowled stubbornly.

"Will you at least turn around?" I asked.

He did, and I looked for the speaker but didn't see anything.

"If you really did know me and who I'm with, you wouldn't bother with a stupid fence and guns. Ask Tucker and Jerry how well that worked for them. We don't want your damn supplies or whatever else you have in your buildings any more than we wanted theirs. I just want to find my parents."

"Can't help you. Leave."

"No. You want me to leave? You'll have to shoot me."

Drav growled very loudly but held his ground.

"And I can promise you shooting me will be the biggest mistake of your life. You don't want to see these guys angry."

"We already have. Two of them took out three units in less than a minute."

I didn't believe him. Ghua would have told us about any altercations when he'd returned. The fey weren't shy about killing or talking about it. I opened my mouth to call the disembodied voice out on his lie then remembered the two exiled fey.

"The two that attacked you aren't with these guys," I called out. "Those two are outlaws, the men these guys have been looking for."

"Yeah right."

"What part don't you believe? That these guys have outlaws, just like we do, or that they are looking for the outlaws, much like our own FBI looks for high-profile criminals?"

Silence answered me.

"Throughout the history of our world, fear and intolerance of differences have led to countless wars, segregations, and violence. That world is dead. We don't need to repeat the old world's mistakes in this new one."

"What do you want?" the voice said, finally.

"For you to listen and try to understand. These men have been here longer than any of us. In fact, we are descended from their people. They have been locked away beneath the surface for thousands of years. The quakes from our drilling released this shit storm on us. Not them. They had nothing to do with the hellhounds coming here or the attacks by the two men they have been hunting.

"Since I've met Drav, the man holding me, he's kept me safe from all of it. The infected, the hounds, even my own people. You have no valid reason to ask us to leave, other than fearing what's different."

The bay door to the largest white building rolled open, and a uniformed man strode out. He walked part way to the gate.

"Old world or new world, I can't just give you another safe zone location and risk countless lives because you say your intentions are good. You want us to trust you? You need to prove you aren't like the other two."

"How?" I asked.

"Jerry and Tucker told us about the supplies they left behind with Bud. We have seven vehicles ready right now. Some of these demons can help us retrieve the supplies. The rest can tell us more about their race. How many there are. Where they come from. And just how fast and strong they are."

"First, they aren't demons. They're fey, like from our legends. Second, do you really think they should tell you all their strengths and weaknesses and get your supplies for you just to prove they're trustworthy?" I gave a harsh laugh. "You've got this so backwards it's just sad. You should be the ones proving you're trustworthy." I lowered my voice and glanced at Drav, who still held me.

"Let's go."

He turned, more than ready to take me away from what he perceived as a threat. The man stopped us.

"Fair enough. You help us with the supplies, and I will help you find your parents."

Drav stopped walking and looked down at me.

"I don't trust him," I said, honestly. "He's dressed like some branch of military. Last guy like that tried to shoot me in the head to save me from you."

"Yes. But without his help, how will we find your family? Your surface is much larger than our caverns."

I sighed. "Can you put me down? It's hard to negotiate when you're carrying me like a child."

"This is how you carry children?"

"Sometimes. Are you going to put me down?"

He considered me a moment then did as I'd asked. I immediately faced the man by the building.

"Drav and I can't make this decision alone. We'll need some time to discuss it with the rest of our group."

"We leave in ten minutes."

"Fine." I looked at Drav. "We better hurry then."

Drav picked me up, ran back to the trees, and started speaking to Molev before I even knew what was happening.

"The man said he knows where Mya's humans are and will tell us if we protect them while they get supplies from Bud's house."

"That's not what he said." Both men glanced at me.

"That's what he meant," Drav said.

"Are you against us protecting them, Mya?" Molev asked.

"No. I'm against them using you, and you guys getting hurt in the process."

Molev grunted. "Let's go talk to this human."

The whole lot of them, including Timmy, came with us when we returned to our previous position not far from the fence. The man inside hadn't moved.

Molev stepped forward.

"My name is Molev," he called.

"I am Commander Willis."

"In exchange for helping us find Mya's family, I will send half my men to protect your people while you gather your supplies. The other half will remain here to protect Mya and Timmy until our men return."

"You have yourself a deal, Molev."

Molev turned toward his men. "The supplies stay with Mya and Timmy. Kerr, will you go?"

Kerr nodded and stepped to one side. More men joined him until the group seemed roughly split in half. From within the fence, the sound of engines roared to life. Huge military trucks, like the ones that had evacuated us from the dorms, pulled out from the white building behind the Commander.

"Be careful, guys," I said as the gate rolled open.

"Be safe, Mya," Kerr said.

The rest of the fey stood back while the trucks rolled through. Kerr's group of fey fell-in around the vehicles, keeping pace with an easy jog. I turned toward the gate as it started to close and only made it a step before a gun was lifted and aimed at my head.

Drav growled low behind me, his hand resting on my shoulder.

"What the hell? We had a deal."

"The deal is that they prove we can trust them, and we help you find your parents. We never said we'd let you in."

Had it only been me, I wouldn't have cared. But we had Timmy.

"It's too cold for a four-year-old to sleep out in the open."

"We'll find you a tent." With that, the commander turned and walked away.

Byllo watched me. The look in his eyes said he'd rip down the fence and get whatever I thought Timmy needed. The little boy in Byllo's arms watched me with solemn eyes, too. I gave them both a reassuring smile.

"We'll be fine. Let's find something to eat and drink. Then, I have a surprise for you both. Do you know how to color, Timmy? I bet Byllo doesn't."

* * * *

Timmy and I squeezed into the tent while Drav and Byllo stood outside. Having them so close was a comfort, but I would have rather had them be able to stay in the tent with us.

I finished tucking Timmy into one of the sleeping bags the others had brought with us then lay down beside the boy. His eyes remained locked on me as he sucked his thumb. I stared at him, too, so he would know I was awake and watching and, hopefully, feel safer because of it. Gradually, his blinks became long and heavy until his eyes finally stayed closed and his mouth grew slack.

After pressing a kiss to the boy's brow, I crawled out of the small popup tent. Drav offered his hand and helped me to my feet while I looked around. The sky had darkened considerably since I'd gone into the tent. Most of the men lay in groups on the ground, apparently at ease with sleeping in their clothes under the stars.

"Is everyone settled?" I asked.

"Yes, Mya. Is Timmy asleep?" Byllo asked, his bright yellow gaze on the tent.

"Yeah. Just."

Byllo continued to watch the tent.

"If you think you can squeeze inside, you can check on him."

Byllo nodded and crouched low to unzip the tent and crawl inside. He barely fit.

"Are you ready to sleep?" Drav asked me, his voice carrying through the night.

I shook my head.

"I need to visit the bushes first," I said softly.

"I will take you." He threaded his fingers through mine and led me toward the copse of trees a fair distance from where all the fey men had bedded down for the night. The same exact spot I'd visited a few hours ago in daylight. Now, the light from the fenced-in area barely reached this far.

I released Drav's hand, ready to step into the trees on my own, but he stopped me with a hand around my wrist.

"No, Mya. I will check it first."

I stood on my tiptoes to press a quick kiss to his lips.

"Okay. But please hurry because I really need to go."

He walked into the trees, disappearing for several long minutes during which I bounced on my toes. When he finally emerged and gave me the go ahead, I rushed into the darkness without another thought.

The struggle with my button gave me a moment of worry before I dropped my pants and squatted. I tried to pee quietly so I could still listen. It proved impossible, though. Commander Asshole was going to get an earful when I saw him tomorrow. Had he even given one thought to what it would be like for a healthy human female outside the fence? Probably not when he simply needed to unzip and wave it around to relieve himself.

A breeze stirred some dead leaves behind me. I frowned and turned my head. No breeze touched my skin. A dark shape moved in the trees with me. I opened my mouth, ready to scream when another shape came from behind me. I struggled to finish my business as the two collided with barely a sound. The disgustingly familiar wet sound of a head being removed heralded the end of a threat. How many times would this man need to save me?

Shaking, I quickly zipped and buttoned then flew at Drav as the body fell to the ground. He tossed the head aside and turned just in time to catch me in his arms. I didn't hesitate to pull him down for a kiss. He bent willingly toward me.

My fingers touched matted hair. A tiny alarm went off in my head. That alarm grew louder as the man stiffened at the first press of my lips to his.

I jerked back, almost falling into the puddle I'd made. He caught me with an arm around my waist and pulled me upright before releasing me. We stared at each other in the dark. Well, he probably stared, I could barely see the outline of him.

"You're not Drav," I said softly.

His teeth flashed white then he just disappeared.

"Mya?" Drav said from further away. "Did you call me?"

I stumbled toward the sound of Drav's voice. He caught me in his arms, and I clutched him tightly.

"What is it? Are you hurt?"

"No. An infected was in there."

He growled and picked me up, quickly removing me from the trees.

"It's dead. A fey killed it. I thought the fey was you." I looked up at him feeling slightly sick. "I kissed him."

He stopped walking and looked down at me.

"I thought it was you," I said again, my voice catching.

"Shhh." Drav leaned his head against mine. "Do not cry. We will find who tricked you, and I will remove his head."

I sniffled and half-laughed.

"You can't. He would die."

"I will not share you."

"No. I don't want you to either. I think I startled whoever that was as much as I startled myself when I realized it wasn't you. He took off as soon as I released him. As long as you're not mad at me, let's not make a big deal about this. It was a mistake. That's all."

Drav opened his mouth to say something more, but never uttered a sound.

A lone howl echoed in the air. Gooseflesh exploded on my arms, and I stared up at Drav, panic coursing through me.

He picked me up in his arms and ran toward the fey.

TWELVE

An alarm immediately blared from the military base.

"Condition Alpha! Hellhounds!"

A set of lights inside the fence went dark with a loud pop followed by the sound of broken glass hitting the ground.

The fey, who had been lounging moments ago, jumped to their feet.

"Don't shoot the fucking lights!" someone yelled from inside.

The three remaining lights went out rapidly, plunging everything into darkness.

Drav growled and didn't stop running until he reached Timmy's tent. I set my hand on Drav's chest, seeking comfort while trying to figure out what the hell was going on.

Around us, a soft blueish glow emerged from the dark as the fey's crystals began to come to life. The fey stood ready, studying the darkness. My gaze shifted toward where they watched. My eyes adjusted quickly, picking up the dark shape of the trees and the distant building across the road. I realized I saw far more than I thought I should have been able to see.

Over the ringing of the siren, I heard the men yelling from inside the fence.

"Meyrs, get the replacement bulbs. Davison, get the

ladder."

"I knew we couldn't trust those grey skinned bastards!"

"We aren't shooting out the lights," I yelled back before turning my face toward Drav. "Are we?"

"No."

"Bullshit," an angry voice called behind us. "This is a fucking arrow shaft. We use guns."

"Find them," Molev shouted.

Several groups of fey ran off into the darkness surrounding the camp just as another howl ripped through the air, barely audible under the siren's wail.

The idiots were already dealing with hounds and possibly the two outlaws. They needed to shut the siren off before the infected came, too.

Byllo emerged from the tent, holding a very frightened Timmy. I reached out and patted the boy's back.

The sirens stopped. In the distance, an eerie howl rent the air followed by a chorus of others.

"Sounds like they found us," I said softly. I worried for the fey who'd left. They had spears and bows while the humans behind the fence had guns and didn't trust us.

The growls grew louder. The group of remaining fey tightened their circle around Drav and Byllo. I stayed still in Drav's arms, trying to hear over the pounding of my heart.

Drav and Byllo's gazes searched the dark, watching for the telltale flicker of red against the black of night. Off to the side, toward the trees, I thought I saw movement. But nothing emerged.

Pops sounded behind us, and I flinched. The fey looked unfazed.

"What are they shooting at?" I asked.

"A hellhound approaches from the other side."

As soon as Drav said the words, I spotted a dark shape trotting from the dark. The flashes of light that punctuated each pop of a fired bullet didn't faze the beast. Either the shooters were missing or the bullets hitting its flesh didn't faze this hound, just like the one back at the stadium. With its gaze focused on the shooters, the monster growled low and charged the fence.

Six fey moved to intercept. I clutched at Drav in fear for them as the guns continued to fire.

"Stop shooting!" I yelled.

The fey didn't wait. They ran at the beast while the Commander yelled for his men to hold their fire. The gunfire quieted before the hound clashed with the first fey. Grunts and growls filled the air as the fey struggled to grip the beast. The hound sunk its teeth into a man's arm. The other fey used the distraction to impale the hound with a spear and pin it to the ground. The bitten man punched the beast in the throat, still fighting for release.

Another howl came from the trees to our right.

"How many are there?" I asked, my eyes moving from the thrashing hound to the trees.

"I hear three. Do not fear, my Mya. No harm will come to you or Timmy."

As he spoke another dark figure crept out of the woods. Its glowing red eyes seemed to lock onto mine. Dread formed a murky pool in my stomach. The hound lowered its head as if getting ready to charge.

Six fey broke away to face off with the second hound.

Before they could reach it, another beast stepped from the barren undergrowth. This one growled loudly and sprinted toward the fight.

Three of the fey jumped forward, trying to tackle the beast. The other three stalked the first hellhound, waiting for it to charge. It didn't, though.

The burst of gunfire flared nearby us, and I ducked my head. When I looked up, I saw that the hound near the trees was trying to creep around the fey. The beast's eyes were locked on Timmy and me, but the fey kept blocking the hound's attempts to go around. As the hound snapped its teeth in warning, another lone howl came from the darkness.

"Shit," I said under my breath.

"Get those lights working!" someone yelled from inside the fence.

The dozen men fighting the hounds wouldn't be enough. I'd seen how a pack of hellhounds could slowly peck away at their numbers. Numbers we couldn't afford to lose. While the main group of fey stood around Timmy and me, the rest struggled. They needed to help their men.

"Drav, Timmy and I have to get inside. We'll be safer there and the rest can go help."

The tussle of Timmy's black hair moved in the blanket Byllo had wrapped around him. Byllo's gaze met Drav's, and Byllo nodded before he sprinted for the gate.

Drav pressed a kiss to my temple and followed. At the gate, the humans posted as guards lifted their guns, aiming it at Byllo and Timmy. The fey roared at them.

"Lewis. Eldridge. Hold your fire," a loud voice barked from behind them.

The guards immediately averted their weapons. However, no one moved to open the gate when Byllo reached it.

"You have to let us in," I yelled, only a little behind them. "The fey will be able to focus on the hounds better without Timmy and me out here."

The commander nodded sharply, and the gate rumbled open just enough to let Byllo slip inside. Drav and I quickly followed.

While Byllo took Timmy further in, I asked Drav to stop. We watched the fight outside the fence.

Some of the fey who had guarded us had split off toward the downed hellhound. The first spear had snapped, and a second spear held the hound in place as the men continued to stab the beast repeatedly. The thing didn't stop growling or trying to bite them.

"Why isn't it dying?" I asked.

"Our weapons do not kill them."

His words sent a spike of fear through me.

I thought back to the hounds I'd seen Drav fight on the surface. He'd run while both of them still moved. Likewise, I hadn't witnessed what happened to the hounds who'd chased us when we met up with Kerr before returning to Drav's home. Did that mean the hounds couldn't die in the caverns or up here?

The group of fey fighting the two hounds to the right kept the creatures at bay while the rest worked to try to kill the pinned one. My gaze swept the darkness, searching for more glowing red. They were out there, somewhere, along with the groups of fey who had left to hunt them.

A flash of movement drew my attention to the left. A fey

had caught the crazed animal by its neck, reached around, and ripped its lower jaw off in a disgustingly familiar move. The hound continued to make sounds and struggled to lunge for the fey as if unaware it could no longer bite.

The fey fell upon the beast, hacking at the creature. I wanted to turn away but couldn't. It was brutal to watch, but they had to find a way to kill it. If they couldn't, there was no hope for us humans.

Something slammed into the fence right in front of us, jolting my attention. The volume of the hound's snarls competed with the sound of its claws against the fence as it tried to climb its way in. Drav stepped back and growled in return. The men around us opened fire until the hound bled from multiple wounds. The report of gunfire didn't cease, each bullet mangling the beast's flesh further until I could see inside of it.

A light flashed in the dark cavity of its body. Not a normal bright light, but an unnatural dark glow. A shiver raced through me as the sinister non-light shimmered again.

"Did you see that?" I said to Drav.

He grunted.

"Keep shooting at its chest," I said. "Where the heart should be."

Tissue disintegrated under the fire until I saw bone, and the dark peeked through the mangled mess.

"Molev, look at its heart," Drav said.

Molev and another fey rushed forward. The firing stopped, but the hound didn't. It continued its attempt to claw its way through the fence unaware or uncaring of the two men approaching. The fey crashed into the wounded hound and knocked it over. The hound tried to jump back up, but Molev threw his arm around the beast's neck, pinning it while keeping a safe distance from its snapping jaws.

The second man plunged his hand into the creature's chest cavity.

"Hurry," Molev barked.

The fey tugged twice before finally jerking back and pulling out a rugged, black rock from the hound. The object pulsed with its darkness. The hound continued to struggle, unfazed by whatever they'd removed.

"What is that?" I asked.

"It looks like a crystal," Drav said.

Molev strained to keep his hold, the muscles in his arms and neck bulging.

"Break it," Molev said.

The fey wrapped his hands around the stone. His arms flexed and the crystal on his wrist flared blue. With a crunch, the black stone dissolved to black dust, and the hellhound stopped moving in Molev's arms.

"Their hearts are their life crystals," Molev bellowed. "Remove them, and destroy them."

While he tossed the dead hound aside and got to his feet, the fey dealing with the speared hound ripped out the same black stone and crushed it as well.

The floodlights flared to life behind us. The remaining hellhounds yipped and ran back into the night.

The relief I felt in the destruction of the two hellhounds didn't last long, though. With the light, I could see the men. The hellhounds had left their marks on so many of the fey. So had the bullets of the humans within the fence.

"Put me down, Drav."

He'd barely done as I'd asked when some asshole pushed him from behind. Drav pivoted, facing the man.

"What the fuck do you think you were doing?" the man shouted.

"I accept your challenge," Drav said with deadly calm.

"No, you don't!" I quickly tried to step around Drav, but he held me back with an arm.

"No challenge issued, right?" I insisted, looking at the man.

The guy didn't take the hint as his challenging gaze stayed locked on Drav.

"Fuck if there wasn't. You almost got us killed. Why? To prove you could kill the hounds?"

"What are you talking about?" I demanded. "You assholes hid behind this fence while the fey did all the work. How does that translate to them almost getting your cowardly asses killed?"

The man held up several broken arrows.

"They took out our lights and brought the hounds."

"Enough," Commander Willis said, striding toward us. "Go check the back fence." He held out his hand for the arrows. The man surrendered them and walked off stiffly.

The Commander looked down at the broken shafts.

"We use guns," he said.

"And they use spears and arrows. So what? I've already told you, they have two outlaws up here. Those arrows weren't fired by these fey, right here."

"And you expect me to believe it was their outlaws?"

"Expecting anything in this world seems pretty pointless, but I'm telling you the truth. These fey have traveled by day to avoid the hounds because of me and Timmy. They wouldn't shoot out lights and risk us. And none of this would have been an issue if you'd let us in the fence where you could have clearly seen what we were doing, which was trying to sleep on the hard ground."

The commander sighed, a soul-weary sound, and scratched under his jaw as he looked at the bodies of the fallen hounds.

"Infected we can handle if there aren't huge waves of them, but those hounds...nothing we have slows them down, aside from a well-thrown grenade. But they're usually already out of the way before it detonates."

He faced me.

"Collect any supplies you have and bring in your injured. We'll set you up in the training gym. We don't have enough beds for you all, but we've got a good supply of cots."

"Open the gates," he called.

While the fey helped their wounded inside, Byllo joined us. Timmy was still draped against the man's shoulder, one little hand resting on Byllo's neck.

"Are you okay?" I asked the little boy.

He shook his head.

"Did those dogs scare you?"

He nodded.

"Me too. But we don't have to sleep outside anymore. We'll be safer inside, okay?"

He nodded once more, and I wondered if he had any hope of growing up normal.

"This way," the commander said when the men were inside.

He led us toward one of the larger buildings, stopping

soldiers along the way with orders for them to round up all the unused cots and bring them to the training gym.

When we arrived, a few cots already waited.

"We house traveling families or groups seeking shelter until we can get them to a better equipped base. Rest up. We'll talk in the morning. More soldiers will be in with cots."

After that, the man left.

The fey spread out, the wounded taking the cots. I searched through our bags for the first aid supplies and went to work cleaning cuts, bites, and the occasional bullet hole. Drav followed me around quietly, not trying to stop me from using what we'd gathered.

While I worked, Molev spoke to a couple of groups who nodded and went outside.

"Where are they going?" I asked Drav as I dabbed a cut over a fey's eye.

The man held himself completely still and kept glancing at Drav. They'd all done that. I didn't try to send Drav away, though. Having him near comforted me, even in the midst of the fey who I knew would protect me to the last man.

"To guard the entrances. Molev does not trust the humans here."

"I don't blame him."

I added a bandage and stepped back from the injured fey.

"The cut probably needs stitches, but I don't know how to do that. Keep an eye on it. If it starts oozing anything nasty, tell me." It was the same thing that I'd said to all of the fey I'd treated.

I turned, looking for anyone else who needed help. The men lay spread out on the cots that had slowly appeared, courtesy of the commander. Those without cots sat propped against the outer walls. Most already slept. No one else seemed to require my attention.

My eyes burned with the need for sleep, and I shuffled closer to Drav, leaning into him.

"Come," he said.

Drav led me over to two cots pushed together and encouraged me to lie down. I didn't need much encouraging.

"Stay with me?"

"Of course, my Mya." He lay beside me and held my hand.

I drifted to sleep with his thumb rubbing up and down the back of my hand.

*   *   *   *

"Commander Willis will want to know more about the hounds and how to kill them," I said before taking another bite of my plain oatmeal.

Byllo sat at the same table as Molev, Drav, and me. He carefully fed Timmy each bite from their shared bowl. Once the boy chewed and swallowed his current bite, he immediately opened his mouth for more. I was pretty sure Byllo hadn't eaten anything yet.

"He saw how to kill them. The humans do not have the strength," Molev said.

"Sure. We know that. But, it'll take a while for them to come to that same conclusion."

As if mentioning the commander had summoned him, the man walked through the door. As he strode across the room, he addressed Molev.

"Your people can continue to rest here until the patrol returns with the supplies. Meanwhile, I'd like to discuss a few things with you."

Molev's gaze shifted to me briefly before landing on a few of the fey.

"Azio and Ghua, come with me."

The two fey stood and walked out with Molev and Willis.

I finished up with breakfast and glanced around the room. The fey were resting, Timmy was in good hands under Byllo's watchful eye, and we weren't under any immediate threat.

"I wonder if there's anywhere to shower," I said, looking at Drav. The bathrooms attached to our building just had toilets and sinks.

"Most of the humans here smell like soap," Drav said.

I grinned.

"Then let's see if we can find one."

I stood, and Drav followed me outside. I asked a soldier watching our building where I could find a shower. The man led us to a different building.

Inside, not far from the entrance, the soldier opened the door to a locker room type space. He pointed out the stock of supplies and the towels that filled a shelving unit just inside the door, then left with the warning that he'd check on us in ten minutes.

Drav and I took a quick shower together. It felt good to really clean myself, but I hurried to rinse and dry, not wanting anyone to walk in. Especially not with the healing bite still on my shoulder. Once dressed, we left the shower room.

I thanked the man, who'd waited just outside the door, and Drav and I went to rejoin the others in their dining hall.

The fey we'd left there no longer sat at the tables quietly eating a meal I knew they found disgusting. Instead, the bowls had been collected and stacked on one unoccupied table while the majority of the men gathered around a different table. Human soldiers were crowded in with the fey, all focused on something I couldn't see clearly.

Shouts of encouragement and a low murmur of conversation echoed in the room as I pushed my way forward, through their numbers, already suspecting what I'd find.

Four fey sat on one side of the table with four humans on the other. Each pair had their hands clasped above the table's surface. Grins plastered the participant's faces.

"Go!" one of the humans yelled.

The men were at a standstill for several seconds until the first fey grunted. As one, the fey began pushing back on the humans.

Sweat dotted the forehead of each human. Several bicep muscles quivered with effort. They didn't stand a chance. Not in arm wrestling. Not in any physical sport against the fey. In short order, each fey brought his opponent's hand to the table. The fey grunted and grinned while the pairs shook hands. The contenders switched out so four new sets could test each other's strengths.

At the end of the long table, Byllo sat with Timmy. In front of Timmy waited an open coloring book and a couple crayons. Byllo had a crayon in his hand and followed Timmy's gaze to the men arm wrestling.

Timmy twisted in his seat and mimicked the men further down the table, lifting his tiny elbow on the table and held his hand out for Byllo to take. Byllo set his crayon down, gripping the toddler's hand.

Timmy grunted loudly just like the men further down the

table. Byllo grunted and let Timmy knock his hand down to the surface. Timmy's delightful laughter filled the room, catching the attention of the other fey. Soon more fey and even some of the humans came over and "challenged" Timmy.

I smiled. Maybe there was hope that human and fey could co-exist, after all.

Thirteen

The distant rumble of engines and a growing commotion outside our building woke me. Drav's cot beside me lay empty but still retained his heat. Whatever was going on had woken him, too.

I got up and stepped outside while redoing my ponytail. Many of the other fey stood near the building's entrance, blocking my view. Nudging my way through, I found Drav near the front. I stood behind him and took in the sight of the busy enclosure.

Human men poured from the white building and ran toward the fence where the gate was in the process of sliding open. Just beyond the outer fence the convoy of seven vehicles, along with their fey escort, approached. No infected trailed behind them.

The vehicles and fey cleared the gates, and I smiled at the sight of Kerr's familiar face. With Drav at my side, I hurried toward the gate to welcome the fey back. The commander already stood nearby with Molev.

While the humans looked tired and dirty, the fey appeared well enough and no dirtier than when they'd left. They'd fared much better than we had.

Kerr saw us and jogged over.

"How did it go?" Molev asked.

"Bud is dead. I'm sorry, Mya," Kerr said.

"Can't say I'm really sorry about that. He was an asshole. What happened?"

Kerr shrugged. "When we returned, the gate stood open. A trail of cans led from the empty barn into the woods where we found Bud's remains and several waiting infected. We cleared the infected and helped gather the supplies the infected had left in trails all over the woods."

I didn't like the sound of that. More baiting and traps. Drav's fingers brushed over my side in a comforting gesture.

"Was anyone hurt?" I asked.

"No. One gun misfired, but the human survived."

"Misfired?"

Kerr nodded.

"If you will excuse me," the commander said, "I need to talk to my men."

The four of us watched him retreat into the white building with the driver from one of the vehicles. The gates closed and the men, human and fey, began to unload the supplies. I hoped the commander would deliver on his promise after talking to his men. We'd delivered on ours.

"What happened?" Molev asked Kerr.

"One of their men shot at me while we were clearing the infected. When I said I accepted his challenge, he said it was a misfire. An accident. It was not, but I kept the peace," he said, meeting my gaze.

I smiled at him.

"I bet it wasn't easy, but thank you for not giving Commander Willis a reason to withhold information from us.

Hopefully, we'll find out where my parents are soon."

"And more women?"

"I hope so." Except for me and Timmy, uninfected women and children seemed pretty scarce. "I'm going to go check on Timmy and make sure he's been fed," I said.

"Byllo fed him twice already. The child was hungry during the night. He's sleeping again," Molev said.

Drav walked with me back to the building, and I stopped to peek in on Timmy. The little boy slept curled against Byllo's side on a single cot. The fey just lay there, eyes open, watching the entrance of the building. When he saw me, he nodded.

"Timmy ate and relieved himself then wanted more sleep."

"That's just fine. Kids that age might still need naps, but I'm guessing everything he's going through is just taking a little bit more out of him."

Byllo frowned, concern on his face.

"Taking what out?"

"It's just an expression. It means he might be more tired than normal."

Byllo grunted, and I left the pair to gather the supplies the fey had brought inside our first night. With nothing left to do but wait, Drav and I returned to our position near the gate. Molev still watched the soldiers.

"No news yet?" I asked.

"Willis has remained in the building," he said.

The newly acquired supplies disappeared into the reinforced shed, and the trucks were parked inside the white building before the commander finally stepped out and strode toward us.

"There's another safe zone in Missouri," he said without

preamble. "Whiteman Airforce Base. Your family is there."

Hearing those words squeezed my heart in the best possible way. Mom, Dad, and Ryan. Finally.

"We've radioed them and shared what you did for us," he continued. "They're expecting you."

He held out a folded map with the route already marked.

"Avoid the places crossed out. There are too many infected there to go in for supply runs."

"Thank you, Commander Willis," Molev said.

The commander gave a slight nod and walked away.

"Ready to head out?" I asked Molev.

"Yes. Lead and we will follow, Mya," he said with a glance at the map.

Drav scooped me up, and I smiled.

"Tell the men we're ready then. And tell Byllo to try not to wake Timmy when he picks him up."

The fey retrieved our supplies from where we'd left them inside the building. Within minutes, we were on our way north. The clearly marked map showed we needed to head up Highway 69, but not to go into the city of McAlester itself.

"Molev, we need to leave the highway before we reach the next town," I said as our group sprinted over the blacktop.

He called out for the group to slow and came over to look at the map with me. I pointed out the area that defined the city of McAlester and the highway cutting through it. Then, I drew my finger along the back roads that would take us far out of our way.

He considered the map in silence for several moments.

"Humans fear the infected because they can become infected. We cannot. You cannot. We are strong, silent, and fast. I think we should stay on your road and go through the city without stopping," Molev said.

"I'm not just worried about Timmy and me; I'm worried about you guys, too. Half the men from last night are still healing, and the commander marked it as heavily infected."

"We will be well, Mya. My instincts are telling me to go through."

I glanced at Drav.

"Molev is the strongest and oldest because he has good instincts."

They both waited for my decision.

"All right. I trust you guys." I reached up and gently traced the scar running across the bridge of Drav's nose. "But, we need to be careful."

He kissed me softly, and a moment later, our group continued toward the city. For the first stretch, we passed wide areas of grass and trees and quiet industrial buildings.

I watched the road and the structures around us. Knowing that the infected had evolved enough to try to bait humans worried me. I could ignore cans of food or a lone figure in the distance, but what if they tried using a kid again? I couldn't ignore that. Thankfully, I didn't see any sign of humans from the highway.

"Do you hear that?" Drav asked softly, still running.

"What?" I strained to hear what he had. Nothing but the whisper of boots against blacktop reached my ears, though, until we approached the city's shopping district. The faint wail of a car horn drifted on the light breeze.

Within moments, a shopping center came into view on our right. In the parking lot, an RV sat in the middle of a swarm of infected. The vehicle rocked as the creatures slammed into the sides, trying to get in.

Molev lifted his arm, and our group slowed.

"It's probably a trap," I said softly.

"Yes," Molev agreed. "But the infected seem to want whatever that thing is."

"It's an RV. A mobile home that people use when traveling."

"So there might be humans inside?"

"Yes. Hopefully, healthy ones."

A scream rang out, proving that uninfected humans were trapped inside.

"We need to help them," I said.

Half the group split off, racing toward the motorhome. The infected didn't notice the fey until the first infected's head flew through the air. The horn quieted, and the infected turned as one, attacking the immediate threat to their existence. It didn't matter that the infected now worked together. The herd of at least seventy infected posed no challenge for the fifty fey. Blood bathed the exterior of the RV by the time the last one fell.

In the silence, the fey watched the camper. The door stayed firmly closed.

"We need to go down there, Drav. If there are humans inside, the sight of you guys is probably scaring the hell out of them. They'll never leave the RV."

Drav grunted and led the way from the highway to the parking lot. The fey moved out of the way so Drav stood near the front of the group, just on the outskirts of the dead bodies now surrounding the RV. The stink of rotting flesh almost made me gag before the wind shifted, bringing cleaner air.

"Can you put me down? I look more like a captive than a willing…" What was I? I glanced at Drav, and found him watching me knowingly.

"I look more like a captive than a girlfriend."

He smiled slightly and let me down. With a blush covering my face, I focused on the camper.

"I really hope you're not all infected in there," I said in a normal voice. "And I really hope you can hear me without me needing to yell because I don't want any more infected chasing us."

One of the windows slid open an inch.

"We can hear you," a man said. "And no one in here is infected."

"Good. What happened? Why are you here?"

"We're on our way to the McAlester Ammunition Plant and stopped for supplies."

"The commander from McAlester said they don't come here because of too many infected." As I said that, I heard a distant call. A moan like we'd heard on the road when the infected had tried to ambush us.

"The infected know you're here. Can you start the RV?" I asked.

"No. We came out with supplies, and it wouldn't start. Something got to the engine."

A trap.

"We need to get out of here. You have two options. Stay in there and face the infected on your own, or come out and let these men carry you out of the city."

"What are they?"

"They are the men who can hunt and kill infected and the hellhounds."

"You going to McAlester?"

"No. Whiteman. Honestly, McAlester isn't that safe. We just came from there. They had a hellhound attack the night before last. The whole thing would be filled with newly made infected if these guys hadn't been there."

The door opened, and a young woman with greasy blonde hair stared over her shoulder while the other inhabitants started yelling at her to close the door.

"I'm fucking tired of this shit," she said, not addressing us. "Everything wants to kill us. She's cleaner than I am and standing there telling us these guys are safe. Either they are or they aren't. Either they kill us or the infected do. I'm done."

She faced us and saw all the infected bodies for the first time.

"Holy shit."

"Yeah, stay where you are," I said.

I glanced at the men around me. Most of them had infected blood on them.

"Same rules apply to these humans as Timmy. If you have infected blood on you, stay away."

Some of the men grumbled, and others chuckled.

I looked at the girl again.

"If it's okay, one of these guys will carry you. They can run much faster than we can."

"Sure. Whatever."

I called out the names of a few men who had been around me enough that they weren't overly weird.

Ghua, still clean, stepped toward the girl first and picked

her up.

"Hi," she said nervously, looking up at him.

"I will keep you safe," he said.

She exhaled shakily. "I'd really like that."

An infected called out again, sounding much closer.

From the shadows, another girl stepped forward. "I don't want to die here."

"How many are inside?" I asked.

"There's twelve of us, total."

"We need to hurry. Molev, who else can carry someone?" I asked.

Drav scooped me up, and Molev started calling out names. When a woman with a young girl stepped forward, I knew the woman wouldn't want to be separated from her daughter.

"It will be harder and less safe if one of these guys tries to carry two people," I said before she could ask. "But whoever carries your daughter will stay right beside you the entire time." She reluctantly handed over her whimpering daughter and squeaked a little when the next man picked her up effortlessly. She glanced at me, and I gave a half smile.

"You'll get used to it."

The human men were last, hesitating on the steps.

"We can walk," one said.

"We don't have time for that," I said.

An older man with white hair nudged the other man out of the way.

"Speak for yourself. If one of you wants to carry me, I'm willing to take the lift."

I grinned and watched Azio move forward to pick up the man.

"Azio, be extra careful. Humans with white hair tend to be more fragile."

The older man snorted.

"Come on, Mary, your chariot awaits," the man said.

An old woman stepped down and looked over the men.

"Oh my," she said. "I don't think I've seen this much bare chest since watching the Summer Olympics."

I chuckled, already liking Mary and the older man.

An infected came from around the side of the RV. The already bloody fey moved to create a protective circle around the humans and beheaded the infected.

"That's so gross," one of the girls said, turning her head away.

"Gross but effective." I looked at the remaining human men lingering by the RV. "It's now or never."

In short order, each of the twelve RV inhabitants occupied the arms of a fey. The group set off at their normal sprint, heading north out of town. A few of the fey hung back and dealt with any infected that tried to follow.

Once we cleared the city limits, I asked Molev if we could stop. He immediately lifted an arm and the group slowed.

"Good instincts, by the way," I said, giving his arm a pat after Drav placed me on my feet.

He nodded, and I turned to the humans who the fey were also putting down.

"My name is Mya. This is Molev and Drav."

The mom stepped forward. "I'm Jessie and this is my daughter, Savannah. Savvy for short." She went through the rest of the introductions quickly, nodding toward the older couple first. "That's James and Mary, then Finley, Ollie, and

Aaron." Each man raised a hand when she spoke his name. The girls did the same. "And that's Hannah, Emily, Taylor." They all looked close to my age. The two remaining boys, Caden and Connor, looked about twelve or thirteen.

"Thank you for helping us," Jessie added.

"I'm glad we found you. You're welcome to travel to Whiteman Air Force Base with us. We were told my family is there."

"Yes. We'd like that."

"Good. Byllo, can you bring Timmy's bag and let Jessie use some of the wipes to clean up Savvy?"

He brought Timmy over to the woman, and another fey followed with Timmy's supplies. While they quietly cleaned up the kids and got them something to drink, I motioned for the other humans to move a little further away. The fey stayed loosely positioned around us. Drav and Molev remained with me. There would be no private talk to help explain things.

"Drav found me the first night this craziness all started. He didn't know a word of English then but kept me safe. Through all of it. The hellhounds, the infected, the bombs. I'm not telling you this so you trust him. I'm telling you this so you understand why I trust him and the others. Why I'll take their side over yours if it comes down to that."

Aaron slowly shook his head at me as if I'd lost my mind.

"They will keep you safe as long as you don't do something to jeopardize my safety or the safety of any other woman or child," I said.

"Why just women and children?" Aaron asked.

"Because they don't have any of their own."

"Seriously?" Taylor said under her breath, looking at the

146

fey with partial awe.

"Yes. They'd never seen a female until me or a child until Timmy. This is still very new to them."

"So they are stealing women and children?" the older woman asked, horrified.

"No. I'm not stolen and neither is Timmy." Technically we kind of were, but I wasn't going to get into that. "We were both rescued. They're helping me try to find my parents. Along the way, they're also looking for any humans who aren't infected. But, I'll be honest. They're mostly interested in any female who would be interested in them."

"You mean interested-interested?" Taylor asked.

I nodded.

"Drav and I are very happily together. The rest see what Drav has with me, and they're hoping for the same. They are kind and gentle. They will ask you if you want to be carried...unless you're in danger. Then you don't get a choice. They are loyal and very protective. But they are also a little clueless about some things. Because of that, we need to set some rules so there are no misunderstandings."

"Jessie, you might want to cover Savvy's ears. Timmy, too," I said to Byllo. As soon as the children's ears were covered, my gaze swept over the fey. I knew what I needed to say, but could already feel my face heating.

"Humans are typically modest. We like staying covered, so no asking..." I swallowed uncomfortably. "No asking to see someone's pussy. And no more using that word."

"What word should we use?" one of the fey asked.

"Nothing. You don't need to talk about that part."

"Then how can we ask to see it?" another asked.

"You don't!"

There were unsatisfied grumbles around me, but I ignored them and addressed the humans once more, my face burning.

"These men don't know much about us or our culture. But don't mistake their naivety for lack of intelligence. If they do something that makes you uncomfortable, tell them. Nicely. If you're rude to me, they take offense. Don't use nasty words or slang. Not only are there children present, but these guys take things literally."

The girls, including Jessie, continued to watch the fey with a mixture of doubt and fear. I turned my attention back to the fey. Other than their open, hopeful expressions, they didn't have much going for them. Infected blood covered the majority of them. If I wanted the new girls to look at the fey in a different way than they did now, I needed to figure out how to get the guys cleaned up. But, first I needed to finish the rules so they didn't ruin their chances before they even got started.

"Any female under the age of eighteen is completely off limits for anything other than respectfully keeping her safe. Humans are still considered children until eighteen."

I glanced at the twelve newcomers.

"Do any of you have any questions about the rules?" Most of them shook their heads. "No? Good. Any fey with questions can ask Drav privately." I didn't want to deal with their pussy complaints.

"Now, we need to find a place for these guys to clean up."

"We're out in the open, and you want to stop for a shower?" Aaron asked angrily.

Savvy, who'd been dozing in her mother's arms, jerked

awake with a cry.

The old man hushed Aaron; and Mary moved closer to Jessie, who held her daughter to her chest and bounced the child, trying to ease her back to sleep. The dark circles under Jessie's eyes stood out, another indicator of her exhaustion as her bounces became slower.

"Jessie, dear, give me the girl for a bit. Let one of those handsome men carry you for a moment or two," Mary said with a wink.

"I will carry you, Jessie," echoed around us as many of the fey spoke up at the same time and stepped forward.

The woman immediately took a step back and clutched her daughter a little closer.

"Back off boys, please," I said stepping forward. "We'll get the guys cleaned up first. But, maybe in the meantime, we can all walk. With this large of an escort, we're safe." I gave Aaron a pointed look.

The group surrounded around the humans, and Jessie moved over to where Byllo walked with Timmy in his arms.

FOURTEEN

The humans we had saved continued to be wary of the fey and tended to stay as far away from them as they could. That meant the group was spread out in its plodding pace with the humans in the center. Caden and Connor, the young teenaged boys, dragged their feet against the ground in exhaustion. The girls walked in a group, leaning on each other. Jessie struggled to hold her daughter, changing her from hip to hip in an effort to find relief. And, Mary and James had fallen behind the rest.

We'd already walked for a couple of miles when we came up to a large lake. The water looked murky, but I didn't think the men would mind. The humans needed the rest, and the fey needed to bathe in order to continue carrying them.

"This is a good place to wash up," I said to Drav.

He grunted in acknowledgement and set me down.

"Are we going to rest for a bit?" Ollie, one of the older men with tired eyes and grey at his temples, asked.

"Yeah, we can rest while they wash up."

The fey who walked at the front dropped their pants without warning and went into the lake. The trio of girls gasped. Hannah's eyes went wide, but she didn't glance away. Taylor just gawked. Emily squeaked and turned away. Then she squeaked again.

I turned around to see more of the fey men pull the strings to their pants and drop them where they stood. Those standing near Mary looked at her before confidently and slowly walking past.

"Oh my!" Mary exclaimed as she got an eyeful. Most of the fey smiled proudly at her examination.

"Mama!" James called.

"Oh hush it, Pa. This is good for the blood." She winked and continued staring at the men who walked passed her.

Drav growled behind me.

"What?" I asked, turning around to him. He stood, watching the others walking naked to the lake.

"I do not like you looking at the others."

I smiled slightly and stepped close.

"Drav," I framed his face with my hands. "I only want you." I pressed a quick, chaste kiss to his lips. "And, as I recall, you had no problem with me seeing their bathing when we were in Ernisi."

He grunted, and water splashed as more fey made their way into the water.

"So stop worrying about what I'm not even remotely interested in and give me something I do want to look at."

He smiled and wrapped his arms around my waist.

"Join me?"

I glanced over at the brown water and the steam rising from the men already washing. I was no fool. That lake had to be as freezing as their underground river.

"I think I will pass."

Drav grunted then stepped back to pull off his shirt and drop his pants. I shook my head at his shameless walk into the water.

"You're a lucky woman," Mary said, ogling Drav's firm butt as he walked away.

"I am."

Mary's eyes went big as one of the fey left the lake. The afternoon light caught on his wet, chiseled chest.

"Mary," the fey said acknowledging her.

"New rule. No flirting with married women," I called.

"Oh, hush," Mary said.

"What is married?" a fey called.

"It's when two people are committed to each other and no one else."

"How do we know if a woman is married?" another fey asked.

"Married women usually wear a ring on the third finger of their left hand. If in doubt, politely ask if she's married."

A few of the freshly bathed men strode past the girls. Taylor nodded to them, taking their bath in stride. Jessie, who sat near Byllo, Timmy, and Savvy, kept turning her daughter back to her coloring book instead of the parade of naked fey.

The human men stood off to the side, talking quietly and ignoring the fey who had stripped down and washed off.

I walked toward them, curious about what they were so quietly discussing.

"We need food. The women haven't eaten in days. I know Jessie gave all of her rations to Savvy," Finley said.

Aaron hushed him and stared at me. I moved away from their conversation and went to the water's edge to wait for Drav. He, Molev, and I needed to talk. There wasn't enough food in my bag to feed everyone. We only had enough small portions to last Timmy and me a day. Just enough time for us to reach Whiteman, according to the map that the commander had given us.

Drav saw me, dipped underneath the water, then started toward shore. He emerged, water trickling down his body as steam rose from his skin. My mouth dropped open a little as I stared. He'd definitely given me something to look at. He was mine. All mine. My chest tightened as my eyes dipped lower. When I looked back up, Drav's eyes locked onto mine, and he smiled.

I tried to suppress my own smile and shook my head at him. I had to keep my thoughts on the humans who needed us, not the delicious expanse of Drav on display.

Unable to resist, I peeked one more time as he walked toward me. I licked my lips in appreciation, and he rumbled in satisfaction at my response.

"We need to focus," I said, stepping back as Drav stalked toward me.

"I am."

He stepped closer, his body brushing against mine.

"What did you want to talk about?" he asked, leaning in to kiss the side of my neck.

I shivered at the feel of his cool lips on my skin.

"Mya."

"Huh?" I was too distracted by his lips to remember his question.

Drav laughed quietly as his lips continued to blaze a path to my mouth. When he reached my lips, I made a sound of agreement and tugged my fingers through his hair, bringing him closer. His tongue traced the seam of my lips then delved inside, making me forget time and place. Only the two of us existed, and one of us had too many clothes on.

He pulled away, and when I finally opened my eyes, he wore a proud grin on his face.

"That was some kiss," I breathed.

"Did it help ease whatever worry filled your mind."

"Huh?"

"You came over with that look in your eye. What was troubling you?"

I shook my head, trying to gather my thoughts that had fled with his kiss.

"The humans haven't had anything to eat for days. We need to feed them."

Drav looked over my shoulder, and I turned to see Molev standing dressed behind us.

"Small groups can go out and scout for houses with food," he said.

I considered all the potential problems with that plan. The fey knew cans had food in them. But, they wouldn't know what kind of food because the fey couldn't read. While we didn't really have any right to be picky, I wanted to at least try to avoid feeding our new friends dog food.

"It would be best if each group took a human or two with them while gathering the food. Someone able to read the labels."

"We will take the human men."

I looked over at the younger boys, Connor and Caleb. I had already explained to Molev and Drav that they hadn't come into their manhood. Although I didn't want the kids out there, sending the older men worried me. It took most men time to warm up to the fey, and I didn't want anyone doing anything stupid while out scavenging.

"Maybe it would be better if I went out with a single group. If we don't collect enough in one trip, we could go out again."

"No, Mya. That would take too long. We will take Connor, Caleb, Ollie, and Finley. We will protect them."

"Okay. But, be careful. And, no challenges while you're gone."

"They will not be gone long, Mya."

I nodded. While Molev went to speak to a few of the fey, Drav quickly dressed. By the time he finished, four groups of five fey had split off to speak to their assigned humans.

Connor and Caleb enthusiastically listened to the fey who explained the boys' roles in the hunt for supplies. When two of the fey turned around so the boys could climb up their backs, neither boy hesitated.

Not everyone in the group was as excited as Connor and Caleb, though. With a worried frown, Jessie watched the boys leave. Byllo reached over, set his hand on her arm, and spoke quietly to her. She nodded and rubbed her daughter's back as the girl colored with Timmy.

Finley and Ollie didn't get the same consideration the younger boys had. The fey told them they needed their help then threw the men over their shoulders and took off.

Some swearing trailed in the group's wake.

"Where are they going?" Hannah asked, stepping over to where I stood with Drav. Shax joined us, studying Hannah avidly. Interest sparked in his gaze.

"They're going to gather food," I said.

155

"It's not that we aren't hungry, but it's getting later. Are we going to be traveling at night?"

"No. We'll probably need to make camp somewhere."

Shax moved closer to Hannah, inhaling deeply through his nose. Her eyes cut over to him.

"What are you doing?" she asked warily.

"Smelling you. You smell different from Mya. But still good."

"Excuse me?" Hannah said, taking a step back.

Shax shadowed her move.

I smothered a grin at her expression.

"Think of it as their way of flirting," I said, trying to ease her worry.

Hannah's eyes went big as her gaze darted between me and Shax.

"Sniffing is flirting to them?"

"I am Shax," he said before I could answer.

He stood inches from Hannah. His hair, wet from bathing, stuck close to his neck, its length just brushing his shoulders. Hannah's hair was about the same length but in tight ringlets. Shax lifted his hand as if to run his fingers through the curls.

Hannah took a quick step back.

He tilted his head to study her, not at all bothered by her retreat.

"You have no penis," he said.

Hannah made a pained sound and glanced at me for help.

"Shax, that's not something we like having pointed out. We're very aware we're not made the same as you."

Hannah quickly retreated, and Shax stared after her.

"Did I say something wrong?" Shax asked, still watching

her.

Hannah joined the other human women, who were moving closer to Jessie.

"You might have come off a little strong," I said.

"What does that mean?"

I patted his arm.

"It means no more penis talk."

Shax's gaze swung back over to Hannah. Determination lit his eyes. I cringed, wondering what he would do next.

Drav, who'd quietly watched the exchange with me, laughed and wrapped his arm around my shoulder.

"The men will not stop," he said.

"I know. Just trying to give them some pointers."

While we waited for the raiding parties to return, the rest of the fey spent the afternoon attempting to converse with the women. Mary willingly talked to each fey who spoke with her. She seemed to understand their curiosity about females and didn't appear to fear them like the other girls. Any time one of the fey approached one of the younger girls, they only responded with short, quiet phrases.

Drav and I remained nearby, ready to keep the fey in check. However, none of the fey pushed too hard with their flirting. Their attempts ranged from the obvious, "you have boobs" to the men challenging each other to brawls in front of the women.

Byllo ended up taking Timmy, Jessie, and Savvy to the edge of the lake, away from the commotion. The remaining human men stood back and watched the fey as well.

As the afternoon dragged on, I began to wonder what was taking the fey so long to scout for food. I tried to see the positive in the delay. With so much time together, the other women gradually grew more relaxed with the fey's presence. However, the fact that none of the groups had returned by the time the sun touched the horizon worried me.

James and Ollie, the oldest of the men, began walking the edge of the area. They picked up small branches and made a pile of them near the center of our gathering. It made sense that we'd want a fire once the sun set and the night turned cold. We humans would need the warmth. That thought just made me worry more. Would the fey know that Caden and Connor would need extra warmth?

"The sun's almost down. Where are they?" I said to Drav.

"Do not worry, Mya. They will return soon," Drav said. "I can hear the young ones."

I followed the direction of his gaze. The group was walking the road in the distance, with Ghua at the front. Caleb sat upon the shoulder of one of the fey.

When the group reached us, the fey pulled Caleb from his shoulder and set him to the ground. The boy beamed with happiness and pride as he raced toward his friends. He barely reached the others before he started telling his story.

"Zoihm went first into the house we found and just chucked out a zombie's head. Then Hanno ran in to help, but Zoihm had taken care of all the zombies waiting inside. Once it was clear, we all went in. The guys let me pick out the food. Said I was the only one who could." Caleb spoke fast, pointing to the fey. "Hanno said they aren't hungry. That means there's enough for all of us to eat."

The other groups slowly began to return, too. Although the food they brought back wasn't abundant enough to feed the whole group, it would feed the people the fey had saved until we reached Whiteman. The humans lit the fire and started warming cans of food over the low flames as night descended.

The fey spread out in a protective circle surrounding us. Those who'd gone out to scout for the food lay down to sleep while those who'd remained behind stayed awake and vigilant. Both sets quietly watched the humans eat, listening and learning, and likely thinking of their possible futures with one of the girls.

The fey were finally living, not just existing.

FIFTEEN

A plane flew overhead. While the other humans gave relieved laughs, I worried. I'd witnessed the destruction those planes could bring, if they chose, and thought their presence more of a warning than a comfort. I didn't know how the people of Whiteman would receive us.

My gaze tracked the progress of the plane until it disappeared up into the clouds.

"How much further, Mya?" Mary asked.

"According to the map, we should only have a few more miles to go."

"That's a shame," she said. "I rather enjoy being carried."

I glanced at the fey who currently held her. He winked down at Mary, and she giggled.

"Woman," James called, "don't forget who you're married to."

She grinned and winked at her husband, who smiled back.

The speed of the fey ate up the miles quickly, and only a few minutes later, we heard the faint reports of gunfire. The men immediately slowed down.

"We need ten who are willing to scout ahead," Molev said. "I will lead." Nine other men stepped forward, and Molev nodded to Drav before taking off again.

The men continued to carry us, but they walked, letting Molev's group scout ahead. No one complained about the pace or continued protection.

It didn't take long for Molev's group to return.

"I think the sounds are coming from the place we want. It is a fence that stretches very far. Men dressed like those with Willis stand inside the fence. Infected surround the barrier. The humans are using guns to shoot them, and the sounds are drawing in more infected."

"Did you see a gate or a way in?"

"Yes."

The hesitation in his eyes made my stomach dip.

"What aren't you saying?"

"They are many people at Whiteman. There are even more infected outside."

The worry congealed in my stomach, and I looked off in the direction of the base. We were so close.

"We should bait them like they've been baiting us," Ollie said.

"What do you mean?" I asked.

"They're still distracted by sound, right? Let's get a car or two and race up to the gate. Honk the horn. Rev the engine. Whatever it takes to get them to follow the car. Lead them away so the rest of our group can get in."

Everyone else got excited about the idea while I dwelled on Ollie's words.

"Wait," I said, looking at Molev. "The infected are attracted to sound. They have been since the beginning. The military would know that. How many infected bodies are laying outside the fence?"

"None. The bullets are missing their heads."

I glanced at the humans.

"You think they brought the infected to the gate on purpose," James said, watching me. "Why?"

"Exactly. Why? We helped McAlester during a hellhound attack. If not for these guys, the McAlester safe zone would be filled with infected already."

"How do we know it isn't?" Aaron said. "All we have is your word that you helped. Maybe that's why Whiteman is blocking its gates. Maybe they know you didn't help. Maybe these guys are the spread of the infection."

"Keep talking like that, and I'm going to tell that nice man to drop you on your head," Mary said with a scowl and a pat on her own carrier's arm. "You just ignore him. We know you helped."

The fey grinned at her.

"So what do we do?" Jessie asked.

"I'm not sure. What if Aaron's right? Not about our help, but about their doubt of it? Maybe Commander Willis didn't let them know we were coming like he said he would. Maybe the plane that flew overhead saw us headed toward Whiteman and told them a large group of grey-skinned people was headed their way. How did you feel when you saw these guys? If Whiteman wasn't warned, they're probably feeling the same way."

"If you helped, why wouldn't that commander share the information? I saw what those hounds can do. Bullets didn't seem to bother them. If these guys can take care of them, we need their help," Taylor said.

I rubbed a hand over my face, wishing I knew what to do.

"Mya," Molev said. "We can get you inside."

"How?"

"The infected are easy to kill. We will leave you here with—"

"Nope. Not happening," I said. "They have guns, and I don't trust them not to use them on you. If you're so sure that you can clear the infected, then I'm going with you."

"Us, too," James said.

"Safety in numbers," Emily added.

Jessie looked at her daughter and Timmy before meeting Byllo's gaze.

"I will keep you all safe," he promised.

She smiled at him, a telltale blush spreading across her cheeks.

"We go together, or we don't go at all," I said, looking at Molev then Drav.

When no one else said anything, I took a settling breath.

"All right. Let's do this."

Molev assigned an extra man to each human. Shax moved beside Drav with a nod to me.

"Protect the humans," Molev said. "Even from their own."

A shudder ran through me at his words. I really hoped it didn't come to that again.

"You will be safe," Drav said, pressing a quick kiss to my temple.

"I know. But will you?"

With a signal from Molev, the group started on our last stretch. Anticipation and worry battled in my stomach. I desperately wanted to see my family again but not at the expense of Drav.

The firearm discharges grew louder and more frequent as we neared. The little ones covered their ears and looked scared, but they didn't shed a tear or make a sound. Ahead, the fields gave way to a road then grass leading up to the long length of zombie lined fence, just as Molev had described.

The gate, what I could see of it, looked like a dual system. A long, wide channel of more fence separated the exterior gate from the interior gate. Both of them were firmly closed.

As soon as we came into view, the gunfire stopped.

In the sudden quiet, the infected lost some of their drive to claw at the fence. The forward push from those still arriving slowed then ceased. The almost silent thump of the fey running over the earth drew the attention of the infected.

They began to turn toward us.

"Do not stop!" Molev yelled.

The sound of his voice started an infected charge. The mass of them poured toward us, crashing into the fey at the front of our protective circle. Without pausing, the fey ripped off heads, clearing a path toward the main gate. Bodies fell, and the fey ran right over the top of them.

Drav held me tightly, sprinting toward the place of supposed safety. A place still firmly closed to us.

"Mya!"

I barely heard the voice over the noise of the infected and shouts of the fey. Through the fence, I caught sight of people running toward the group of uniformed men impassively watching us.

"Open the damn gate! There's people out there. Kids!"

The cried demands from inside didn't change anything.

With the gate still firmly closed, the fey fought their way

through the infected. Once the first of the fey reached the metal barrier, the men spread outward, killing the infected trying to press in at the sides. The forward momentum didn't stop until those of us in the center stood at the gate, a half-circle of fey protecting us.

Most of these infected didn't seem as smart, their movements not as coordinated. However, a few groups worked together, targeting a single fey and trying to pull him away from the rest. The other fey didn't allow that to happen. They kept the infected at bay, beheading one after another in a bloody spray of gore.

A hum filled the air, and the outer gate began to move. Byllo rushed through with Timmy first then the fey who held Savvy. Drav waited until all of the fey carrying humans had wedged their way through before he moved forward into the press of bodies. Slowly, the remaining fey followed. I saw the problem right away. We wouldn't all fit. Still, the rest of the fey backed toward the opening, keeping the infected from reaching us.

The hum filled the air again, and the outer gate began to close.

I twisted around in Drav's arms and looked at the men. They had their guns poised, ready to fire. But at who? Us? The fey still outside? The infected?

"If they start firing on the rest of our group, we need to stop them," I said softly to Drav.

"Yes."

The outer gate barely closed when the inner gate swung inward.

"Move quickly!" a man shouted.

Drav tensed. I waited for the first bang to sound. Instead, a man stepped forward and started waving for us to hurry.

"Move!" he said again.

Byllo sprinted forward, the rest of us following. But not far. A circle of heavily armed men surrounded us. Drav stopped and turned back. We watched Molev and the rest continue to fight. My pulse raced as an infected bit down on his arm. The last fey ran from the space of safety between the two gates, and the inner gate swung shut.

I looked back at the men with the guns then Molev. The man shoved the infected back and ripped off his head before turning and dealing with another.

The outer gate began to hum once again. The remaining fey backed into the opening, a solid front against the infected. A garbled yell came from within the mass of milky-eyed bodies, renewing the frenzy of the creatures.

"Get in position!" someone yelled.

More men ran forward, passing around our guards to stand five feet from the fence, their guns aimed at the infected and the fey now trapped between the two gates. The fey didn't stop fighting until the last infected within the enclosure with them fell to the ground.

No one opened fire on the infected still outside the fence. The gate didn't open either.

"Timer!" someone yelled.

"Three minutes," someone called back.

"Put me down, Drav," I said.

He started too, but a shot into the air and a yell stopped him.

"Do not move!"

I looked over his shoulder anyway to the man who was doing all the yelling.

"What the hell are you doing?" I asked. "They just killed a quarter of the infected out there."

"And they were bit. Some of you could have been bitten, too. Timer," he said again.

"Four minutes and thirty-seven seconds," another man answered.

"So you're waiting to see if some of us will change? These men won't. Didn't Commander Willis contact you?"

"He did. And I surely hope that these fey men can do what he said they could."

For the next eleven minutes, we all just stood there with guns trained on us. I honestly didn't mind so much because, beyond the lines of men with weapons, there were lines of people fearfully watching us. The guns were meant to protect them, the survivors.

"Time's up!" the man with the watch yelled.

There was a long moment of silence then the inner gate made a noise and swung open for the remaining fey to enter the base.

"Now, which of you is Molev?" the man in charge asked.

"I am," Molev said, stepping forward.

"Welcome to Whiteman. You and your men are sorely needed. Will you follow me so I can explain our situation?"

"No," I said before Molev could move.

"No?" the man asked.

"Who are you? And, where are my parents?"

"I'm Matt Davis."

"No title?"

"None that would really matter anymore."

The way he said it set a lead ball in my stomach. As bad as it had seemed out there with the infected getting smarter, I'd hoped that was just my skewed perception. Having someone in charge of a safe zone say something like Matt just had, meant we were as screwed as I'd thought.

From the sea of uniformed military personnel, two people rushed forward.

"Mya!" my mom yelled.

Drav immediately set me on my feet.

"Mom! Dad!" I ran toward them, meeting them halfway. Their arms encircled me. Mom sobbed and held me tightly. Dad pressed several kisses to the top of my head.

"I can't believe you're here," Mom said, pulling back to look at my face.

"Me either," I studied her just as hard, memorizing the new worry lines creasing the corners of her soft brown eyes.

"Where's Ryan?" I asked.

"Cleaning up infected at another gate," she said.

Drav moved behind me, drawing her attention. I realized he had Dad's attention, too.

"Mom, Dad, this is Drav. He's the reason I'm alive. He found me that first night and kept me safe even though he had no idea what I was."

"You smelled good," Drav said.

I grinned and blushed slightly. Mom's gaze flicked between us.

"I see."

"And there are your parents, as promised," Matt Davis said. "If it's all right with you, I'd like to speak to Molev."

I glanced back at Matt.

"They need to clean up first. Although the infected blood doesn't bother them, it could contaminate others."

"I understand your concern," Matt said. "However, I'm hoping they will be willing to leave again. We need to clear the infected from the fence line so we can do a supply run."

"You were using your guns before, use them now."

"The sound draws them in."

"Yeah, which makes me question why you started using guns after your plane flew over and saw us coming."

He glanced at everyone around him then back at me.

"We had to know if what Commander Willis said was true."

"And what did he say?" I asked.

"That these men fought like demons and could kill anything."

"They can and have been. First showers, then talking."

I looked at my parents. Mom still silently cried. Tears of joy that broke my heart a little. I wanted to hug her some more. Both of them. But I knew that Drav and Molev needed me more at the moment. Matt had plans for them, and I had to be sure those plans wouldn't lead to their annihilation.

"I'm so glad to see you," I said quickly. "Let me clean up and listen in on the talks, then I'll come find you."

Mom nodded and waved me off. Dad hugged her.

I turned to Matt.

"These men are not your new weapon. They might be your new allies, though."

He nodded.

"If you'll follow me, I'll show you to the showers myself," he said.

169

The other humans in our group walked beside their newly made fey friends. Matt didn't question their presence, relieving me a little. When we reached a large building, he pointed toward the two labeled doors.

"Ladies to the left and gents to the right," he said. "We converted this building for temporary public showers to accommodate all the families, which you'll see when we tour the zone. It's rustic, but it will do the job. You'll find what you need inside."

"I'll stick with them," I said, taking a step toward the men's room.

Matt started to frown, but I held up a hand.

"You needed proof to trust. I'm no different."

"Fair enough."

I stepped inside and studied the ceiling while giving basic instructions for turning on the showers, adjusting the temperatures, and rinsing away the infected blood.

"Rinse your clothes out, too," I said. "You'll probably need to wear them around wet. Sorry guys."

As soon as everyone finished, we stepped back out into the light. My parents had joined Matt in waiting.

"Mya, I thought you might be more comfortable with your parents showing the rest of your group around while we speak."

Mom gave me an encouraging nod and glanced at Drav again. I turned to Molev.

"You okay with the rest of the men going with my mom and dad?"

"Yes."

I focused on the group behind me. "These are my parents.

170

Remember the rules. No swear words in front of them. No asking the questions you know you're not supposed to ask. No challenges until after you get back. No matter what. We clear?"

A bunch of "Yes, Mya," followed.

"Mom, do you have more daughters?" one of the guys in back asked.

"Are you married to Dad?" another asked.

"New rule. No questions at all until you get back," I said.

"Mya," Mom scolded with a hint of amusement, "they can ask us whatever questions they want."

"No, they can't." I felt on the verge of a heart attack just thinking of one of them asking to see her southern parts using the p-word.

I gave the men a hard look. "I mean it."

Matt cleared his throat.

"Follow me," Mom called. The men walked after her, and I could already hear her talking about the base.

"They will keep her safe, Mya," Drav said.

I smiled and shook my head.

"I know they will. I'm more worried about what they're going to say."

Drav, Molev, and I followed Matt to another building where he had maps pinned to movable boards.

"What is all this?" I asked, looking at the colored pins placed here and there.

"Bombed cities, clusters of infected, fallen safe zones, remaining safe zones, and sightings."

"Sightings?"

"Of the two men you're hunting and of the hellhounds. I

won't go into the boring details of how we know all of this—"

More like he still worried the fey would somehow use those details against them.

"—but I wanted to show you what we face so you understand why we need your help. The black pins are bombed cities. The red pins are fallen safe zones. The green pins are functioning safe zones. The yellow pins are high volume areas of infected. The white pins are sightings. We're here," he said, pointing to the lone blue pin.

Black, white, and red dominated the area around us. McAlester had a red pin in it.

"Commander Willis?" I asked, touching the pin.

"On his way here in an armored truck. The infected breached his fence this morning."

"They're getting smarter," I said.

"They are," he agreed. "But, a bullet to the head will still end them."

"So, what do you need from these guys?"

"Their help. We need to end the most aggressive source of the infection. The hounds know we're here and want in. Without the perimeter lights, the fence is useless to keep us safe. But, if we can eliminate the hellhounds, we might have a chance. Not just here but worldwide."

"Do you know how many hellhounds there are?" I asked.

"We're estimating over one hundred here and almost as many overseas."

I looked at Drav and Molev. Why had it taken them so long to catch onto the fact that eating the deer made them monsters? Sighing, I faced the board again.

"What's the plan?" I asked.

"The hounds hide during the day. Usually in abandoned buildings. We're hoping if these guys go in after them, they can pick them off when they are at their weakest."

"We will help you," Molev said.

"Thank you." Matt's relief showed in the droop of his shoulders.

"I was thinking we could divide your men into three groups to attack here, here, and here," he said, pointing at white pins on the map.

"When?" Molev asked.

"Just after first light tomorrow."

"We will meet you at the gate."

Matt extended his hand, and Molev looked down at it. I reached forward and shook Matt's hand. Matt gave me a surprised look but caught on when he glanced at Molev and found the fey studying our hands. Molev shook his hand after I let go.

Although we'd just reached Whiteman, I knew the world outside the fence wasn't going to give us a break because we were tired and wanted to rest. The fey needed to go. And the fact that I didn't like it one bit didn't matter.

"Make sure the men who go with you come back," I said.

Matt nodded and resumed his study of the board as we walked out.

Sixteen

Mom and Dad were just outside the door, waiting.

"Where are all the fey?" I asked.

"We left them with their friends. They're figuring out the tent assignments. We thought you might want to join them. But, maybe we could talk first?"

"Yes, I'd like that." I hugged both my parents again then followed them as they led the way down a road.

"This part of the base is still used for the planes and pilots and whatnot. Toward the back, in the open areas, the military set up tents for the survivors when this first started. There's a lot of room now," she said sadly. "A week ago, one of those hellhounds got in and killed quite a few people before leaving again. It took a while to clear the infected out. Last night, another hound showed up. It didn't get as many. We all sleep with guns now."

It felt surreal hearing my mom say that.

She continued pointing out areas of interest as we walked our way across the fenced-in base. When we spotted the tents, I saw immediately that the fey had a table set up and were arm wrestling some humans.

I made a noise of exasperation.

"Oh, be nice," my mom said. "It's obvious they are trying

to fit in. And they are so nice."

Dad snorted.

"What?" I asked, suspiciously. "What did they do?"

"Oh nothing. Your father is still miffed that one of them asked to see my pussy."

"Oh, God." Both my worst nightmares had come true. They'd asked the question they weren't supposed to and my mom just said the p-word.

"Mya, don't you dare scold them. It's obvious they're curious about us and are just trying to learn. Here we are," Mom said, stopping in front of one of the drab green tents. She pulled back the flap and motioned for us to enter.

I went inside the square canvas tent and looked around the dim interior. The space wasn't huge by any standards; but there was a small stove to the side for heat, a cot across from it, and two more shoved together against the back wall. As my parents sat on the doubled cots, Drav and I settled on the ground, our backs to the unlit stove.

Guessing the single cot belonged to Ryan, I glanced at the opening of the tent, half hoping he'd suddenly show up. I needed to see him.

"Ryan'll be back shortly. His shift at the gate is almost done, sweetie," Mom said, catching my gaze.

I nodded.

"We've worried about you every minute since the attack. Will you tell us what happened? How you two met?" Dad asked.

"Yeah. I guess I should start from the beginning."

I told them everything but glazed over some of the details of how Drav and I met. My parents listened raptly, not interrupting at all. Mom did sniffle, though, when I told them how Drav and I had been only a step behind them during the week before the bombings started.

Drav grabbed my hand and rubbed his thumb against mine when I spoke of his world and our time there. My parents gripped each other's hands when I described what happened to me at the superstore, and my heart broke at the sight of Mom's silent tears.

She waited until I finished before she slid off the cot and held out her arms.

"Oh, baby," she sniffled against my hair.

"Quite a tale, Sis."

I looked toward the entrance of the tent. Ryan stood there, the afternoon light shadowing his features. Since I had last seen him, shaggy brown hair had been replaced by a short, almost military cut.

I swallowed hard and untangled myself from Mom to rush to my brother. He hugged me hard in return as my hands brushed the rifle strapped to his back.

"I wasn't sure we'd get to see each other again," he said, still holding me.

"Your messages helped. Thank you."

He gave me a brotherly pat then released me. I really looked at him. He had worry lines around his eyes now, too, and he looked much leaner. I tugged him further into the tent.

"How long have you been standing there?" I asked.

"Long enough to hear about your time down under and the trouble you've been brewing since you came back."

His gaze went to Drav, who still sat on the ground.

"This is Drav," I said, taking a step closer to the man who'd stolen my heart.

Drav stood and nodded toward Ryan.

"Sorry about the welcome you received at the gates. But, thank you for bringing Mya to us. For keeping her safe. Keeping her alive."

Ryan held out his hand to Drav. Drav glanced at it, then at my brother, before clasping his forearm. Ryan returned the gesture.

"She is the only good thing up here," Drav said. "I will always keep her safe."

Ryan didn't try to stifle his laugh this time.

"You'll fit in just fine."

Dad stood and repeated Ryan's thanks and handshake. Seeing all the people I cared about finally together warmed my heart.

"So what happened to you guys? I want to hear everything."

We all settled back into our seats, Ryan joining Drav and me on the ground.

"Ryan started talking nonsense about hounds in Germany," Dad said. "He was so worked up, we had already agreed to pack up and head to the cabin before we even heard the first howl. Ryan figured out real quickly that the lights kept those monsters away. We stayed in the house with every light on until after the hounds swept through the city. Then, we loaded up the car, rigged floodlights on the roof, and headed north. We made it to the cabin with no problems. But, it helped that we arrived after the hounds had already gone through."

I nodded. "We saw Doug."

Dad sighed, and Mom made a small sound of grief.

177

"When the military came and told us we needed to leave, that infected were coming, Doug never answered his door. They didn't give us time to check on him ourselves."

I was glad they hadn't. If they'd tried, they might not be alive now.

"The military escorted us to Tinker during the day. The infected were everywhere in the city. They came out in droves at the slightest sound.

"Once we got to Tinker, we searched the crowds for you, hoping you were already there. We ran into some other survivors from Oklahoma City. They told us the same story about the university evacuation that you did. We never thought we lost you, though. You are too smart. But, every day more survivors came, and there was no word from you." Dad swallowed hard. "We tried to stay at the base as long as possible. They were flying out survivors during the day and digging in at night. The whole time, those hounds seemed to know right where we were, attacking anyone they could reach. The military forced us out here two days before the bombings started.

"So much has changed since the bombings. This wasn't the only base the military set up for civilians. The people in charge then had the survivors spread out, living and working in different safe zones. We kept in contact with several of them. Getting reports. Coordinating military efforts. But, more bad things started happening.

"The infected started setting traps. Less military personnel were returning from supply runs. Then, some of the safe zones stopped answering. Flyovers showed them overrun by infected. More convoys of survivors started showing up here.

However, that stopped when the hounds returned a few days ago.

"McAlester was one of the last nearby safe zones. Our long-range communication is spotty. Nothing better was turned back on. From what I know, we have only spoken to Europe once since the world went to hell.

"We don't know what's still left of the world or its leaders."

"What happened to the military leaders at this base? At McAlester, Commander Willis was still in charge. His men seemed like true military personnel. It doesn't seem like that here," I said.

"That's because so many of the people left are civilians. Evacuees. Families who escaped. People who don't know how to be military but still need to do their part in protecting this place. We're all adjusting. We work hard. We're surviving."

We were silent for a moment after that statement. The new world was not kind. The humans here were surviving; but given what Dad had just said, they wouldn't have survived for much longer. This safe zone would have fallen like all the other safe zones. My hands trembled at the thought, and I clasped them in my lap.

Drav and I were here now, and the fey would keep them safe. But, the hounds and the infected weren't the only issues we faced.

Winter was on its way. The weather had gotten colder since we'd returned to the surface. Cold weather meant finding ways to keep warm. The little stove in the tent was a start, but I'd already noticed there was no wood. We would need supplies to survive. We would need to leave the safety of the fence.

"You are thinking very hard, Mya," Drav said, leaning toward me to press his lips to my temple.

"There's a lot to think about."

"There is," Dad agreed.

"How about we go get some dinner? We'll look for an extra cot so you can stay with us, Mya," Mom said.

Drav's hand twitched on my thigh. I set my hand over his, likely thinking the same thing. Seeing my family again had been amazing. I couldn't believe they'd made it here safely. That they were still alive. But, the fey had become more than friends to me. They felt like family, too. And, Drav felt like so much more.

"I'll be staying with Drav and the other fey."

"All right," Mom said with a small, disappointed smile. "Let's go eat. I'm sure Ryan is starved after his shift, and I bet you two haven't eaten in a while."

"No, we haven't."

As the four of us made our way through the encampment, I paid more attention. Everywhere I looked, I saw the same thing. People pushed to the point of exhaustion. They shuffled toward their tent, then the flap closed behind them.

"Where did you go this time?" Mom stopped to ask a man passing us. His lifeless blue eyes stood out against his weary, dirty face.

"We tried for the superstore in Sedalia. Almost made it. Another trap. The infected took out half of our supply party this time." The guy's voice didn't change in pitch while sharing the news.

"Emery?" Mom asked quietly.

"Gone. I kept my promise to him when he was bitten."

The man walked away and closed himself in a tent.

"Who was that?" I asked.

"Emery's father. He's lost everyone now," Mom said.

My parents' words came back to me. *We are surviving.*

Were they? Making through one day to the next, dying a little inside each day? I wasn't sure that counted as surviving.

We didn't stop to speak to anyone else as my parents led us to the mess hall. We joined the line of silent people slowly shuffling into the building.

Further inside the door, a hardened woman stood at the counter, scooping out food to each person who passed by her. Another woman, with a kind smile, handed out rolls.

When my parents reached the stack of trays, they each grabbed one then stepped toward the counter. The woman scooped some kind of steaming stew mixture on their trays. It looked amazing, and I eagerly stepped up with my tray.

With a scowl of dislike, the woman fixed her gaze on Drav.

"Some of your kind was here earlier. Said they'd only eat meat. I got Spam."

"Spam will be fine," Drav said.

The lady grunted, grabbed two small cans of spam from under the counter and plunked them on Drav's tray. She plopped a scoop of stew onto mine.

"Don't mind Bertha," Mom said as we walked away. "There are a lot of people who are having a hard time adjusting, and accommodating everyone isn't possible. She's a little touchy."

"It's fine, Mom. This looks great. Far better than what I've had to eat in a long time."

181

"Don't get too used to it," Ryan said. "This is it until there's a successful supply run."

We sat at an empty table and quietly ate our food. I savored each bite of my hot meal while trying not to pay attention to Drav enjoying his gel-covered Spam. When we finished, we took our trays to another counter where a different pair of women worked, washing their way through a tall stack of dirty trays.

"We all have jobs here," Mom said as we left the building.

"I bet I know what your job will be," Ryan said, reaching out to give my hair a playful tug.

Drav growled.

"It's okay, Drav. Ryan's just teasing me. It didn't hurt."

Drav grunted and gave my brother a warning look. I grinned at Ryan and arched a brow.

"You're not playing fair," Ryan said.

I shrugged and turned to Mom and Dad, who watched me closely.

"Drav and I really need to check on the rest of our group."

I wasn't overly worried about the fey. But, in a lot of ways, they were like children. They didn't know much about the human world, and I didn't want them to get into any trouble.

We found the fey at the far end of the encampment where they had been assigned the tents closest to the fence. With the help of the humans we'd rescued, the men were settling into their new homes.

Savvy and Timmy chased each other. Byllo and Jessie stood together watching the children.

"These men are just amazing with children," Mom said.

"They really are."

"Come on," Dad said. "I'm sure whoever is in charge has a tent for you somewhere around here."

As we walked, I noticed tent numbers and names already written on tape near the openings. Three fey had been assigned to each tent. We kept walking, looking for a tent with Drav's name on it. Before we found it, we found Molev talking to a man with a clipboard.

"Mya. Drav," Molev said in greeting.

"Hey, Molev. What's going on?" I asked.

"We're setting the fey up in these tents by the fence," the man said.

"Why's that?" I asked. I already had figured out the reason, but I wanted the man to say it aloud.

"To protect all of us from the hounds," the man answered.

"And to keep them as far away from the rest of you as possible?"

The man looked down at his board briefly before meeting my eyes.

"I think most of us would take a lion as a house cat if it would keep us safe."

I sighed. It would have been foolish to expect open acceptance. The fey were too different for that. But, I knew after the people got to know the fey, their attitudes would change like mine had.

"Your tent is not by the fence," Molev said to me.

The man nodded. "Tent H11 has been assigned to you and Drav. The H-row is the fourth from the fence."

Drav threaded his fingers through mine as we followed my parents toward our assigned tent. Two sleeping bags and my backpack waited inside by the cold stove.

"This one looks nice," Mom said. "No cots, yet. Your Dad and I will see if we can find you some."

"Thanks, Mom." I hugged them both before they left. A chorus of "Bye, Mom," echoed through the tents.

Ryan grinned at me.

"I better go, too. I have another shift for body removal before I can sleep. I'll talk to you tomorrow. Find me in the morning, okay?"

I nodded and gave him a hug, too.

Drav put an arm around me as we watched him walk away. Byllo, Timmy, Jessie, and Savvy moved to a tent just three down from ours. I smiled when I realized they would be sharing. It made sense. Timmy and Savvy had slept together almost every night since they met.

Mary and James walked around from the tent just in front of ours.

"This is some place," James said. "Big from the sound of things. Most of it's not used because it's too hard to defend. Heard there are some real houses on the other side."

"With real beds," Mary said.

"Would you rather stay in the houses?" I asked, wondering what they were getting at.

"No, no," James said quickly. "We feel safer here."

"But it seems a shame that all those mattresses are going to waste."

I smiled, understanding.

"I'm sure any fey you ask would be willing to take you to a house and get a mattress for you. Maybe even a whole bed. There's no reason for you two to have to sleep on a cot."

"Cot?" Mary laughed. "They gave us sleeping bags."

She was right. Why let good mattresses go to waste? I looked up at Drav, and he started to call out names. The fey immediately jogged over and nodded when he asked if they would help Mary and James.

A group of ten fey left, two carrying the couple.

Since I'd explained marriage, all the fey respected Mary's relationship with James. But they still flirted with her like crazy. I heard several tell her that if she ever got mad at James and desired another, she could come to him. She'd laughed each time and gave the speaker a wink before sending him away so she could eye his backside.

I turned back toward our tent and stared at the clean sleeping bags.

"What are you thinking, my Mya?" Drav asked.

"That I really want a shower before bed."

"A good idea," Drav said, stepping around me to pick up my bag.

We walked to the communal showers where Matt had taken us earlier. Drav held my hand the entire way, neither of us talking. The day's events still ran through my head. The infected at the gate. Seeing my parents. Matt's request that the fey help them in the morning. It still felt surreal that we were really here. That my family was still alive and so close.

As I'd guessed, my family accepted Drav because I did.

At the showers, I took my bag from Drav.

"I better go to my own side this time," I said. I stood on my toes and gave him a light kiss on his lips before entering the women's showers.

By the time I finished, it was dark outside. I shivered at the chill of the air on my wet head.

Drav, who'd been waiting for me outside, noticed the movement and scooped me into his arms.

"You grow cold too easily," he said, already jogging back to our tent.

I snuggled against him while denying his claim.

"My tolerance of the temperature changes is pretty standard for humans. But I'm sure glad you don't get as cold as I do."

Drav ducked into our tent, set me down, and closed the flaps. I looked around in mild surprise. A mattress now took up a large portion of the canvas floor, along with a little table that held a lit glass jar candle. The bed had been made up with real sheets and piled with three quilts.

"I really like Mary," I said, knowing this had to be her doing.

Drav's arms circled my waist, and he held me close from behind. Snuggly in our tent and out of the chill, the heat of his chest pressed against my back warmed me. As did the light trail of kisses he placed from the base of my neck to my jaw, where he stopped.

"Are you happy, my Mya?"

I turned in his arms and looked up at him.

"I am. Are you?"

"Yes." He brushed his fingers over my cheek and down my throat. "With you, I am always happy."

The sincerity in his gaze only made my feelings for him stronger.

"I'm so glad you found me. I love you more than I ever thought possible."

"My Mya," he said, cupping my cheek gently.

His mouth settled over mine in a slow kiss that stole my breath. Each tender touch of his lips melted my heart further.

Wrapping my arms around his neck, I melted into his kiss. He growled softly, and the mood of the kiss changed as he gently cupped my breast with his warm palm. A jolt of desire shot straight through me, and I couldn't stop the small sound of enjoyment that escaped.

Drav pulled back, his thumb brushing over my nipple before he released me and tugged his shirt over his head. Tossing it aside, he waited, his intense gaze asking what his mouth wouldn't.

I smiled slightly and kicked off my shoes. He didn't move. I tugged off my shirt then eased the straps of my bra over each shoulder. His sharp gaze followed the movements as I freed my breasts. My bra hit the floor beside his shirt. Reaching for the clean jeans I'd just put on, I released the button and listened to the rasp of the zipper.

With his focus entirely centered on my hands, I slowly worked the jeans over my hips and saw the moment he realized I wasn't wearing any underwear. The sound of his breathing increased, and I smiled. Naked, I walked to the bed and glanced over my shoulder at Drav.

The hunger in his gaze stole my breath. He tossed his pants aside and strode toward me.

SEVENTEEN

Drav kissed my temple and eased away from me. I rubbed my eyes and rolled to my side to watch him move in the dim light of the burned down candle.

"What are you doing?" I mumbled, still too tired to fully form words.

"I must meet the others by the gate," he said softly. "Rest."

There was no chance of that knowing he planned to leave.

"No. I'm up. I'm coming to see you off."

He sat on the mattress and watched me dress. His appreciative gaze traced over every curve I possessed. I loved the way he watched me. Smiling to myself, I tugged my shirt over my head then stepped into my boots.

"Let's go," I said, holding out my hand.

His fingers curled around mine. Instead of standing, he tugged me down on top of him. I landed with a squeal and a giggle.

"I love the sounds you make," he whispered just before kissing me lightly. "You will make them for me again when I return."

"Bossy," I said, teasingly.

"Yes," he agreed. "You are."

"Hey!"

He smiled and stood with me in his arms.

"I will carry you until I have to leave."

"Fine. But just this once."

He winked at me, and I leaned my head against his chest as he stepped out of the tent. The longer we spent together, the more human he behaved. Just the good stuff, though. The teasing and the laughing. I supposed that made sense. His life before me had been all fighting and surviving.

At the gate, most of the men already waited. Molev and Matt spoke together near the vehicles. No infected waited outside, just the stained, dried grass showing where they'd once stood. A plume of dark smoke rose in the distance.

"Good morning, Mya," Matt said. "That's the clean-up crew's fire."

"Good morning. Any word from Commander Willis?"

"Complete silence, which likely means he is infected now, too."

The man didn't pull any punches with his news. While hearing the information sucked, I also appreciated the complete honesty.

"How long do you expect these guys to be gone?" I asked.

"Everyone should return before dark. Group one will clear a smaller overrun safe zone to the north. Groups two and three will check nearby sightings."

I looked up at Drav.

"You be careful out there," I said.

He kissed my forehead then turned to Matt.

"I want your promise that you will keep Mya safe while I am gone."

189

"You have my word," he said.

I rolled my eyes.

"Drav, he has to keep several hundred other people safe, too."

He ignored me and pinned Matt with his unblinking gaze.

"I will hold you to your word."

"If you're done being adorably overprotective, it's my turn," I said. "Molev, make sure he comes back whole and healthy."

"Yes, Mya."

I tilted my head up to Drav. "Time to put me down."

He kissed me hard and set me on my feet while I was still dazed and grinning stupidly. The gate rolled open, and Drav stepped in with the first group of fey.

I waited there until the last truck rolled through and the groups started off. Drav gave me a lingering look and raised his hand in farewell before sprinting away, his long braids moving in the wind. It wasn't until I turned that I saw Kerr standing behind me.

"What are you still doing here?" I asked.

"Molev needed Drav, not me," he said with a shrug.

"Bullcrap. They left you behind for a reason. Why?"

He didn't say anything.

"Tell me why, and I'll find out which girls here might be interested in hooking up with a hot demon man named Kerr."

"Drav wants you safe," he said immediately.

I grinned, missing that sweet man already.

"Come on, let's go find my brother."

"I thought we were going to find the girl who likes me."

"Patience, Kerr. Girls don't like guys who seem

desperate."

After at least an hour of asking and walking around, we found Ryan by the east gate.

"About time you showed up," he said, catching sight of me.

His dark hair lay plastered to his scalp, and his shirt had sweat stains under the arms and down his chest. He strode over and gave me a huge hug.

"You stink," I said, returning the hug before pulling back.

"I'm conserving supplies by skipping deodorant." He grinned widely.

"And soap from the smell of it. What are you doing to get so sweaty?"

"Just finishing clean up." He pointed a thumb over his shoulder at the dead infected on the ground outside the gate. "We load them up, then the armed group takes them to the burning grounds."

"That sounds gross."

"It is. But it's worse if we leave them lying there. Not only do they smell, but the infected are getting smarter and have started using the bodies to climb the fence."

"Ew. How much longer do you have to work?"

"I'd get done faster if you helped."

"No, Mya," Kerr said immediately.

I rolled my eyes and gave Ryan a shrug.

"I promised I would stay inside the fence."

Ryan looked at Kerr and offered his hand. Kerr took it immediately, surprising me. It shouldn't have though. The fey learned quickly.

"This is Kerr. Drav went out to help clear a safe zone, and Kerr got stuck babysitting me."

"Not stuck, Mya. I volunteered."

"I'm Ryan. I hear you guys are pretty strong and fast. Any chance you want to take over for me so I can spend some time with my sister?"

"Please?" I asked.

"Yes, I will take over. Where will I find you when I'm finished?" Kerr replied.

"Shooting range," Ryan said. He hooked his arms around me and started tugging me along. With a grin and a wave to Kerr, I willingly obliged.

"Why are we going to the shooting range?" I asked once we were out of sight. "And did you even get to sleep last night?"

"I grabbed a few hours. But, there's a lot of work to be done. Which is why you're going to spend some time on the range. You have to be able to shoot to go on a supply run with me this afternoon."

I stopped walking.

"I promised Drav I wouldn't go outside the fence."

"I know. But I also know you'll break that promise."

"Why?"

"I know you've been paying attention, Mya. Even with everyone helping, we're dying here. There aren't enough of us experienced supply scavengers left. If you don't help out, it'll be some kid too young to hold a gun or some older person who can barely walk. We need supplies. You and I have to be a part of those who go, or the people here will starve.

"I get that Drav cares about you. Do you think Mom and Dad don't worry every time I go out? We can't hide behind the fence."

"You suck," I said, knowing he was right. "And Drav's going to be so mad when he finds out."

Ryan grinned, and we continued to the indoor shooting range where he showed me how to use the gun I would be assigned. I wasn't that good, but he told me that with all the infected the fey had killed, there would be less around for the supply run.

When I finished emptying my current clip into the target, I engaged the safety and set the gun back down. Taking off my earmuffs, I studied the odd pattern of holes around the head I'd been targeting.

"When do we leave?" I asked, turning to Ryan.

Kerr stood just behind my brother.

"Where are you going?" Kerr asked.

I shifted my gaze to Ryan, who looked far too amused.

"Ryan, where are we going next?" I asked, hoping the change in wording would ease Kerr's mind.

"Well, you're going to go back to your tent to take a nap like a good little ward, and I'm taking Kerr to meet some of my crew."

I glanced at Kerr. "He means friends."

"Will there be females?" Kerr asked, losing his frown.

"Yep. Not sure they're worth your time, but I'll let you be the judge of that," Ryan said with a shrug.

Kerr grinned widely, showing off his very pointed canines.

"Whoa," Ryan muttered.

Kerr didn't hear. He was busy promising me that he would not ask to see anyone's pussy or boobs.

"You know what? You're with Ryan, now, and his responsibility. Have fun."

I left Ryan with Kerr and started my way back to the temporary housing. I knew darn well Ryan hadn't meant for me to actually nap; besides, the tent would be too chilly without Drav to warm me. But, with nothing else to do, I went there anyway, wanting some time to think.

Around me, people moved with the same weariness as the day before. Some were armed. Some carried things from one building to another. Ryan was right. I needed to pitch in. To help ease some of the strain. Supply runs were a start. After he and I returned, I would talk to Matt to find out what more I could do. Not just me, but the fey, too. These scouting missions were fine, but the fey needed to integrate and become part of the community. Their presence might be what the survivors needed to give humanity hope again.

I'd just reached the tent I shared with Drav when Mom found me.

"Hi, sweetie. Want to come with me and help with laundry?"

"I'm not sure if I have time. Ryan said he wanted me to go with him on a supply run."

Her expression went from happy to troubled.

"Well, if you're going with Ryan, you won't have time for laundry. Promise me you will be careful," she said. "I worry every time Ryan leaves. I understand he has to go, but I still can't stop wishing it were someone else."

I stepped close and hugged her. "I get it. But, we'll be smart and watch out for each other. When I get back, I'll see what I can do to start helping around here."

She hugged me tightly in return then released me.

"You'll need to talk to Matt. He'll add you to the work

schedule."

"I've been wanting to ask, what's the story with him? I know Dad said the military is more relaxed because of so many civilians helping out, but why just Matt and not Commander or some kind of title?"

"We haven't had much luck with people in charge here."

"What do you mean?"

"He's the eleventh leader. All the ones before him have died in some tragic or unnecessary way. Infected. Hellhounds. Suicide."

"Suicide? Now?"

"I know. To make it through so much and then give up." Mom shook her head. "Knowing that something purposely allowed those hellhounds in shook everyone."

"What do you mean?"

"You saw the lights all over this place. They keep the hounds away at night. Over a week ago, someone shot the lights with arrows. The hounds broke through the fence, and well, I already told you the rest.

"Anyway, after that incident, the commander in charge decided living wasn't worth it anymore. There was some dispute about who was next in line. No one wanted to be that person. Matt stepped up and said we needed to change. That military rank no longer mattered. That we were a ragtag group struggling to survive in a world that had either forgotten about us or that had already given up. He said we'd probably all die within a week, but he wasn't ready to give up a day of that remaining time without at least trying. Most of the people agreed we weren't going to make it. But, we all wanted to keep trying."

"How long ago was that?"

"Five days," she said with a sad smile. "Our numbers have been cut in half since then."

Matt had been in charge for four days before we arrived. I thought of his desperation to talk to Molev right away, the maps in his room, and all those color-coded pins.

"When we heard from McAlester that there might be a way to kill the hounds, that help might be coming...well, that lit a new fire in everyone's hearts. Everyone's but Matt's. He cautioned us not to believe in something we hadn't seen for ourselves."

"That's why he drew all the infected in?"

"Yes." She glanced over my shoulder. "Here comes your brother."

I turned to look at Ryan.

"Where's Kerr?" I asked.

"Talking to Julie."

"Oh, Ryan. That poor man will be stuck there for hours," Mom said.

"Who's Julie?" I asked.

"A lonely woman grieving the loss of her entire family. She'll talk to anyone who will listen."

"Kerr said he wanted to meet her," Ryan said.

I shook my head, knowing he'd made the introduction to distract Kerr.

"We better get going," I said to Mom. Now, more than ever, I wasn't going to let Ryan go out alone. I knew what might be waiting out there.

"Be careful," she said.

"We will," I promised. She hugged us both then walked

away.

Ryan and I jogged across the compound. My heart hammered the entire time. I half expected Kerr to show up and tell me I couldn't go. However, Ryan seemed to have found the perfect distraction because we reached the gate without spotting Kerr.

Two military trucks with several armed men already loaded in the backs waited near the gate.

"Thought you weren't going to show," one of the men called to Ryan just as the inner gate swung open to allow the first truck to enter.

Ryan and I jumped into the back of the second one. The man near the back reached out and pulled the metal grate up and pinned it in place, creating a clever cage that would keep us safer from infected.

"Not a chance. Mya, this is Tom."

Ryan introduced me to the rest of the guys in the truck, twelve including us, then asked where we were going.

"Warrensburg," Tom said.

"I thought it was marked," Ryan said.

My stomach sank.

"The town is. But, there's a high school and a few gas stations on the outer edge. We'll scout the school first and if it seems clear, hit it and hopefully find enough food to last us a while."

The truck rolled through the gate, and I looked out at the wide unprotected expanse of field.

I didn't know how far Warrensburg was from Whiteman, but I hoped we'd return before Kerr noticed me missing.

EIGHTEEN

Trees lined the sides of the road, their barren canopy creating a creepy tunnel. No one spoke over the rumble of the engine as we stood in the back, watching the roadsides. Ready for anything, each man had his gun aimed outward through narrow windows in the steel grates.

Nervous energy made me feel twitchy. Yes, I had volunteered for this. The people at Whiteman needed food. And, I didn't want Ryan to go without me, not when I could see how exhausted he and most of the other men were. But, knowing I needed to help didn't make me feel any better about leaving the security of the fence. Drav would be furious with me.

The truck rocked as we hit a pot-hole.

"Is this the safest route?" I whispered to Ryan.

"Nothing is really safe anymore, Sis. You should know that."

Yeah, I did know. Ryan nudged me playfully with his shoulder.

"So you and the big gray dude, huh?"

"Shut up," I whispered, almost smiling. Only Ryan would bring up my love life at a time like this.

"Debris in the road," Tom said, keeping his voice low.

"Watch the trees."

The truck slowed, and I glanced at Ryan.

"We'll probably be able to drive over whatever it is."

A series of pops went off from the lead truck.

"One from the trees," Mark, who watched the front, said. "He's down now."

The rest of us kept our eyes on the trees as the first truck went through whatever the infected had tried to put in our way. Branches based on the sounds. Our truck rolled over the debris next without another infected sighting.

I glanced back at the trunks of the two large trees laying in the road, and anxiety coiled in my belly as we drove on. It didn't feel right that only one infected had been out on its own. Not with that kind of trap laid. The thought that the infected were getting smart enough to not attempt an attack because we didn't stop made me shiver. Hopefully, there was a different route home.

It didn't take as long as I had expected to reach Warrensburg. Other than the trees, we didn't run into any more obstacles.

"Is this the first run to this place?"

"Nah, we've hit Warrensburg before. We went to a preschool the first time. General store another time. We try to pick locations on the outskirts. It's too dangerous to go further in because of the noise of the vehicles," Ryan explained.

It took a few more minutes before I spotted the high school. The large building dominated the surrounding acreage while the parking lot sat barren and ghostly.

How long had it been since students walked Warrensburg High's halls? Around a month now, I figured. School felt like a lifetime ago. Ryan had been a senior. Would he ever graduate, now? I glanced over at him and doubted it. He wasn't that kid anymore, and our new lives didn't require diplomas.

The trucks cruised through the parking lot straight toward the side entrance where they stopped and cut the engines.

"In and out guys and girl," Tom said quietly. "If you see an infected, try to avoid it. If you have to shoot, shoot to kill and get out before more come. Truck one has the cafeteria. We're here for the routine things. Sanitary items. Let's move."

Two of the men quietly opened and lowered the back gate. The first man jumped out of the truck and headed toward the doors, which opened without a sound.

A crackle of static came from the cab as I waited my turn to climb out the back. I glanced at the cab as the driver picked up the radio and spoke quietly. He turned to look back at me through the window.

Tom went around to the driver, and Ryan nudged me so I would get moving. Mark remained, closing the gate and guarding the truck.

I checked the safety on my gun and started toward the side door with Ryan when a hand came down on my shoulder.

"You weren't supposed to come, little lady," Tom said.

It felt like a rock settled in my stomach. A radio call from the base meant that Kerr knew I was missing.

"We need help, right?" Ryan said before I could speak for myself. "We all pitch in to stay alive."

"Just keep an eye on her," Tom said, before moving past us into the building.

Ryan nodded his head for me to follow.

Inside, the lights didn't work. The hall we stood in wasn't

completely dark, but several of the men held penlights and shined them up and down the hall's length. The school looked normal, just empty.

"Look for supply closets near the bathrooms. Grab what you can and get back to the truck," Tom said.

The eleven of us split into two groups. Ryan and I went to the right with three others. If we hurried and got what we needed, I'd be back before Kerr could really freak out. Hopefully.

My group walked down the hallway, one of the men's penlights helping to illuminate the way. Light filtered into the hall from closed classroom doors. We came to a set of stairs.

"We'll go up and start a sweep of the second floor. You two finish up down here. There has to be a bathroom somewhere."

Ryan nodded. I hesitated. I wanted to get back to base quickly. Splitting up would be the fastest way to make that happen. But, it didn't feel like the safest. I looked up and down the hallway. There were no blockades or other signs of infected traps.

"You good?" the guy asked me.

I nodded and watched them slowly make their way up the stairs. Ryan motioned for me to follow, and we started down the hall again. Near the end, where the hall branched off to the left, we found bathrooms and a supply closet. Ryan tried the nob. It didn't budge.

"Shit," he said softly.

A brush of noise came from behind us. I looked down the hall but saw nothing. Neither Ryan nor I moved as we waited to see if the sound would repeat itself.

The sudden pop that echoed through the halls made us both jump.

"Come on." I tugged on Ryan's arm, ready to lead him away from the gunfire.

"It's okay, Mya. In a town this size, there is bound to be an infected roaming in here. Hopefully, it was the guy with the keys to the supply closet."

Several more shots rang through the hallway, followed by a scream that bounced down the halls. Ryan's wide eyes met mine.

"Time to go," he said.

He clicked off his light and held his gun between his hands.

"Which way?" I asked.

Ryan paused, looking down both hallways. At the very end of the one we'd already walked, a person staggered forward, stopped, and turned in our direction.

Ryan switched his grip on his gun and grabbed my hand, pulling me down the opposite hall. A groan echoed after us. I didn't dare look back as we ran side by side.

A door opened just as we passed. An infected lunged out and grabbed for Ryan, the momentum taking them both to the floor. I stopped and aimed at the infected, watching its jaws snap at Ryan as my brother held it back with a forearm to the throat.

I exhaled and pulled the trigger. The boom of the shot rang in my ears as the infected fell to the side. Rushing forward, I hauled Ryan to his feet. He picked up his gun.

"Come on." I grabbed Ryan's arm and pulled him down the hallway.

The sound of staggering footsteps reverberated off the

lockers from all directions. More infected.

My heartbeat pounded in my ears as I searched for an exit. Something moved in the shadows ahead.

Ryan tugged me into a classroom then quietly shut the door behind us. We were silent as we backed further into the classroom. Unfortunately, the room only had small windows up near the ceiling. No exit that way. Unless…I looked at the desks, wondering if Ryan would have enough upper body strength to—

The doorknob rattled. We both lifted our guns, ready.

The door quickly opened and a head poked in. I recognized the face. The driver of our truck. His pained blue eyes swept over us before he limped inside and closed the door. Panting and sweating, he slowly slid down the wall beside the door and sat on the floor.

"Greg?" Ryan said. "Were you bitten?"

The guy looked like hell, but I couldn't see blood anywhere.

"Fuck, I don't know. I don't know." He closed his eyes, wincing.

Ryan kept his gun trained on his friend, but his hand shook.

"It's okay, Greg," I said in a calm tone, keeping my gun steady on the man.

"It ain't. I knew there wasn't somethin' right about just one infected on the road. Shoulda turned around. Fucking shoulda turned around." Greg groaned and wrapped his arms around his stomach before puking.

"What do you mean?" I asked.

"Fuckers followed us here."

He retched again then looked up at me with bloodshot

eyes.

"I can see it in your eyes. Fuckers bit me, didn't they."

"Yeah," I said.

"Then kill me now. End it."

I exhaled slowly.

"Kill me!"

A bang rang out, and I flinched. Red exploded onto the wall behind Greg's head, and a dot dripped down his forehead. Slowly, he fell to the side.

I looked at Ryan, who held his gun pointed at the spot where Greg's head had been a moment before.

"Start making a barrier with the desks," I said, touching Ryan's arm to get him to lower his weapon. "Don't drag the desks. I'll check for a radio on Greg. Maybe we can call for help."

Ryan nodded and lowered his gun. I rushed forward to start patting the pockets in Greg's jacket first. Metal scraped over the tile behind me. I flinched at the sound but didn't scold Ryan. Our position had been compromised when Ryan fired.

Finding nothing in Greg's jacket pockets, I tried his cargo pants pockets. My hand hit hard plastic, and I withdrew the radio.

A low moan came from the other side of the door just as Ryan wedged the first desk against it. Pocketing the radio, I rushed to help him, both of us lifting and stacking desks as the moans increased in volume.

The heavy metal desk that belonged to the teacher still sat over in the furthest corner from the door. I motioned to Ryan to help me move it under the windows. We'd just positioned it there, and he'd stepped on the surface when something hit the door. His eyes went to mine, then the window still just over his head. He lifted his gun and hit the glass. It spidered but didn't break out.

"Shit." He hit it again and again. The mesh in the glass wouldn't give.

He jumped from the desk.

"Tip it over," he said.

We hunkered down behind it, and Ryan glanced at the radio in my back pocket. A fleeting look of hope flashed over his face.

I pulled out the radio and pressed down on the button.

"This is Mya and Ryan. We're trapped in a classroom at Warrensburg High School. We need help. Is anyone there?"

I released the button. Static crackled back. I pressed the button again.

"Is anyone there?"

More static.

"Hello?"

No one responded.

Cold fear coiled in my belly and tears stung in my eyes. Help wouldn't be coming.

I turned to Ryan and wrapped my arms around him, holding him tight.

"I'm sorry, Sis."

"The end of the world isn't your fault."

Ryan leaned his head on my shoulder, and I stroked his hair. It felt like we were kids again, riding out a tornado.

More footsteps shuffled outside the door. Something hit it again. This time hard enough to nudge the desks.

I hugged my brother closer.

"Love you, Ryan."

"Love you, too, Mya."

The moaning and groaning in the hall became deafening as the door opened a bit. A hand reached in, the thick, pale blood-stained fingers gripping the door. I pulled back from Ryan so I could aim my gun. Ryan did the same. Together, we waited for the infected to push through.

We watched the pile of desks slide backward an inch at a time until the barrier fell with a loud crash. Three infected shoved through the door, semi-milky eyes locking on us as we fired. As their bodies fell, more came, tripping over the fallen and making it harder to aim for a headshot. Sweat coated my forehead. I kept aiming and firing.

"I have only one more clip in my back pocket. After that, I'll be out," Ryan yelled.

How many shots did I have left? The implication of the few moments we had remaining hit me hard.

The moans grew frenzied in the hall, and scuffling footsteps escalated as more infected pushed through. Ryan stopped shooting briefly to reload.

I kept firing until my gun clicked. Numb to the reality of what would happen next, I tucked myself behind the desk and listened to the mixture of Ryan's shots and the infected moans. Ryan would turn. I wouldn't. The infected would eat me alive.

The shooting stopped, and Ryan crouched down next to me.

"That's it," he said.

I took in a deep breath and held his hand.

"It hurts," I whispered. "But not for long."

He frowned at me. I didn't know how else to comfort him,

though.

"Someone's calling your name," he said.

"That's not funny, Ryan."

"No, seriously. Someone is calling your name, listen."

I heard it. A voice echoing down the hall as it called out my name. Then, another voice joined in, calling my name, too.

"Mya!"

Hope coursed through me. The fey were here, searching for me. I looked over at Ryan. He nodded.

I stood, drawing the attention of the infected, who'd paused in the doorway at the sound of the voices in the hall.

"Drav," I yelled.

Two of the infected lunged toward us. Unable to think of anything else, I threw my gun as hard as I could. It hit the first one in the head, and he jerked to a stop.

Ryan pulled out a desk drawer and hit the second one with it again and again. Infected blood spattered me at the same moment a roar shook the room.

It was the best sound ever.

Heads flew off of the infected crowding the doorway as Drav tore into the room like a storm. The infected who'd entered because of my yell turned toward Drav. He took their heads in a fury, moving so fast that the first head hadn't hit the floor before the next head parted from its body. Blood coated most of the room by the time the last body fell.

Drav stood in the middle of the mess, dripping with infected blood and looking like an avenging angel of death.

"Mya," he said, looking at me for the first time.

I climbed out from behind the desk and threw myself at him, half-crying, half-laughing, and fully shaking.

He caught me in his arms and held me.

"My Mya," he said again and again as he stroked my hair and kissed my head.

I heard Ryan behind me.

"Thank you, Drav."

Drav growled loudly and released me.

"You should not have let her leave," he roared at Ryan.

I stepped in front of Ryan, ready to defend my brother.

"It's not his fault. I had to come, Drav. I can't selfishly hide behind the fence while other humans go out to get food and supplies that I'll use, too. We all have a responsibility to pitch in if we want to not just survive, but live."

"No, Mya. Matt Davis gave his word that he would keep you safe. That promise was broken. We are leaving. Now."

He picked me up and stalked through the door. I looked back at Ryan, who followed behind us, along with several other fey.

Outside the school, Drav stopped to speak to Molev, who studied me with a frown.

"The school is clear," Drav said. "I will take Mya back while you gather the supplies they were willing to risk Mya for."

NINETEEN

Extreme guilt weighed on me as I lay on our bed, snugly warm in Drav's arms. He hadn't loosened his hold on me all night, which I completely understood. I'd scared him. But, did he honestly think it justifiable to keep me inside the fence when everyone else had to go out?

I tried moving a little.

"No, Mya," he said gruffly.

His words tickled the hair on the back of my neck and sent a shiver through me. The reaction prompted him to groan and kiss the tender spot just below my ear. His palm brushed over my still sensitive nipple.

This wasn't the first time he started something since we'd returned yesterday.

"We can't stay in here all day, Drav."

"Yes, we can." His hand slid down my stomach, and I knew I wouldn't win. I wanted him to touch me as much as he did.

As if sensing my surrender, he nudged me to my back and covered me with his very naked warmth. He stared down at me for a moment while settling his hips over mine.

"You're selfish when you risk yourself," he said softly.

"What do you mean?"

"I've told you, you're the best thing here. Without you, I

have no reason to help these people. Without you, we would return to the safety of the home we know. If you care for these people so much, do not risk yourself."

His words were proof that he'd listened to what I'd been trying to say last night. He'd heard me, but he hadn't agreed. While I might not agree with him, either, I knew better than to push just now. Besides, I could be useful in other ways inside the fence.

"I won't. I promise." I leaned up and traced the curve of his lower lip with my tongue.

His hips pressed against mine and, with a groan, he took over the kiss with the consuming energy of a drowning man. The stroke of his sure fingers started a fire beneath the surface of my skin that blazed just for him. He rocked against me in a slow rhythm that showed his love and passion for me.

For the next thirty minutes, the world outside the tent faded away as Drav proved his need for me.

In a sweaty heap, we lay together afterward. Underneath the blankets, his fingers stroked over the bare skin of my stomach. I lay my head against his chest and traced little circles on his skin with my fingertip.

"I don't want you to stay mad at Ryan," I said softly after my pulse slowed.

"Then he shouldn't have told you to go outside the fence."

"How do you know he did?"

"Because that's what you told your mother, and that's what she told Kerr."

"You do know that I could have said no. But I didn't because I understood what Ryan was saying. We're all taking risks just by being alive, and we all need to help out."

210

"No. Not for things outside the fence. That's why you wanted my people to come here. We aren't as fragile as you. As you pointed out to Molev, the hounds exist because of us. We will take care of them. Your job is to stay inside the fence, so we have a reason to return."

I shook my head and exhaled. "You are stubborn, and I love you."

He kissed my temple. "I love you, too."

"Drav," Molev called from outside the tent. "It is time."

"I am staying today," Drav said, his hold on me tightening.

"No, you aren't," I said firmly. "You've made yourself very clear, and I've given you my word that I will not leave the protection of this fence. Now, it's a matter of trust. Do you trust me to keep my word?"

He sighed and studied my face.

"Yes."

"Then go. We all need you to keep us safe."

"I will leave a few more men today," Molev added through the tent, obviously listening. "To watch over the humans who stay behind and to help with any supply groups that leave."

"Thank you, Molev," I said, holding the blanket to my chest as Drav slid from bed.

"I will meet you at the gate, Molev," Drav said.

"Do not take long. We go further this time."

A moment later, Molev's voice called out a greeting from further away, and I knew Drav and I were once again alone. In silence, I watched him pull on his pants.

His gaze shifted from lacing his leather boots up to me. The hunger in his eyes made me smile.

"Will you come with me to the fence?" he asked.

He held out his hand, and I slid from the blankets, grinning even wider at the way he looked at me.

"Of course I'll come see you off. And I'll be here waiting for you, just like this, when you come back." I held out my arms and did a quick turn so he understood.

When I faced him, he wrapped his arms around me and pulled me to his chest for a thorough kiss.

"I do not want to leave," he murmured as he trailed kisses along my jaw to the side of my neck. "I want to stay here and listen to you pant yes again and again."

An embarrassed flush consumed my face.

"I say stuff during sex?"

"Oh, yes. Many things for different places." His fingers traced my collarbone before he nipped my skin, right below the almost healed infected bite. A tingle of need spread through me, and I almost groaned his name.

"Molev said not to take too long," I managed to say, instead.

He grunted and stepped back from me after one more kiss.

"I'll wait outside."

After I dressed, I walked with him to the gate and waved as the men left. The fey who remained watched me like I was going to climb the fence and go running around screaming for infected to come get me.

"Relax guys. I have no plans to leave. In fact, I'm going to go to the dining hall and see if I can help there. I heard they're going to use the potatoes you guys pulled from the school yesterday. With all that butter from the coolers, my mouth is watering big time."

The fey disbursed when I walked away, likely to find their

own ways to occupy the time.

A few people were already working in the kitchen when I arrived. Some scrubbed pans. Some stirred pots. Everyone seemed to be avoiding the pile of potatoes. I walked right up to the mound, picked up a peeler, and got to work.

While the others finished their various tasks and walked out without an offer to help, my pile of peels slowly grew. A few times, a fey would poke his head in and say hi but never stay long. I knew they were just checking to make sure I was still where I was supposed to be.

I didn't mind the quiet time. I thought about yesterday and the fear I'd felt for Ryan and everyone else in the group. And how I'd felt hearing Drav's roar. I loved that man completely. A world filled with infected and hellhounds didn't seem so scary with him at my side. In fact, it seemed darn right survivable because of him.

Each hellhound death meant a better chance of a future for the remaining survivors. I thought about what that future might look like. Moving to houses where families could live...a family with Drav. It would be hard. This world would never be what it once was, at least not in my lifetime. Yet, the world not returning to the way it was might not be a bad thing.

Out of potatoes, I filled a pot with water and started quartering the spuds. Once I had three pots going, I scooped the peels into another pot and went outside. Mom had mentioned they planned a garden in the back field next year, and I figured the peels would make a good start for compost.

Mom stepped out of the laundry building when I passed and waved at me. Carrying a basket of clean sheets, Shax stepped out behind her.

"Where are you going, Mya?" he asked.

"I'm going to start a compost pile with these peels."

"That's a good idea," Mom called. "Set it up just on the other side of the walking path by the field we started turning."

"Ok."

Shax hesitated to follow my mom.

"I left potatoes boiling on the stove. I'll be right back."

Those words must have reassured him because Shax continued on with Mom. I shook my head and kept going, saying hello to the people I saw on the way. I'd forgotten how far away the back of the base was from the kitchen and wondered if Mom would keep an eye on the potatoes. My arms started to get tired as I walked. The peels weren't bad on their own. The pot weighed a ton, though.

When I saw a lone fey walking toward me from the back of the base, I smiled widely.

"I'm so glad to see you," I called.

He looked surprised that I'd spoken to him. Maybe because he looked like a mess. He had to have just gotten back from one of the group missions. His shirt was torn and filthy. He probably wanted to go to the showers, and I felt guilty for stopping him. But, my arms were screaming for relief.

As we drew closer to one another, I noticed the deep scarring on his face and his throat. Scars made from a hellhound attack by the look of them. Although his long hair covered much of the scarring, I felt bad for him. The fey already had the odds stacked against them because of their grey skin and eyes. Adding scars would make it even harder for the poor guy to meet girls.

"What's your name?" I asked.

214

"Merdon," he said, his voice a rasp.

The name sounded vaguely familiar.

"Would you be willing to help me carry this pot to the back field? It's okay to say no if you'd rather go clean up first."

He blinked at me for a moment then took the pot from my hands.

"Thank you," I said, smiling. "I'll show you where it can be dumped."

He waited for me to lead the way and fell in step beside me. I could feel his gaze on me and glanced at him with a kind smile, wondering how long it would take before the fey stopped being so curious about women.

"Did everything go well on the mission today?" I asked. "It looks like you ran into a little trouble."

He grunted in the non-committal way they liked to communicate, so I tried a different topic.

"Have you seen any girls you'd like to meet? I'd be happy to introduce you."

I stepped off the path and pointed to an area between us and the field.

"I think we can dump the peels right there."

He continued walking right past where I'd pointed. I frowned and hurried after him. The fey had farmed a long time in those caverns and had probably picked up a few tricks. If he wanted to place the peels somewhere else, it was fine with me.

Just a few yards from the fence, he set the pot on the ground and turned toward me.

"Don't you think putting the peels this close to the fence is a little dangerous? I mean, I know there aren't many animals out there now. But once the hellhounds are gone, I think having a compost pile here might attract them."

He tilted his head and studied me for a moment.

"What's your name?" he rasped.

"Mya," I said automatically. How could he possibly not know that by now?

Between one heartbeat and the next, I realized my mistake. The scars. The dirty clothes.

This wasn't a friendly fey from Ernisi. One of the exiled criminals stood before me.

I opened my mouth, ready to scream for help, when he crouched forward, knocking the wind out of me with his shoulder to my middle as he picked me up. In a familiar move, he took a running start at the fence before I could catch my breath. The ground fell away underneath me. A second later, we landed with a thud on the other side of the fence, and he took off running.

Every time I opened my mouth to scream, Merdon bounced me on his shoulder, cutting off my air supply. My stomach wanted to heave as the world sped past beneath his feet.

Drav.

What would he think? I'd promised them all that I wouldn't leave.

The scenery changed. The once dense forest thinned, and Merdon ran next to a road. The pavement blurred under his feet, changing to lush grass. Then, the ground got very far away again. My stomach felt weightless, and bile crawled up my throat.

The fey dropped to the ground and slowed his pace. I lifted my head as Merdon stopped and wood creaked under our combined weight.

My heart pounded in my chest at the sight of an untamed yard. Why would he take me to a house?

He stepped inside and flipped me off his shoulder onto the hardwood floor. I teetered, dizzy. His hands gripped my shoulders tightly.

"You will stay, Mya."

Twenty

Merdon didn't say my name with respect or reverence like the other fey did. I studied his iridescent yellow eyes.

"It would be best if I didn't stay," I said.

He released my shoulders and gave me a nudge further into the living room.

"You will stay. You will listen to us."

Us? Shit.

"Listen to you? What do you mean?" I asked.

"Maybe she is like the stupid humans," a gravelly voice said from the back of the house.

I pivoted toward the source.

A fey stepped down the darkened hallway, his gait unbalanced. His dim outline made him look bigger than any of the other fey. Big enough that his broad shoulders almost brushed the walls as he moved forward.

I took a step back, bumping into Merdon as the new fey stepped into the light.

His hair barely brushed his shoulders, but his body was riddled with scars. Bite marks, bullet wounds, and jagged lines from deep cuts...a map of the brutality he'd suffered since his last resurrection.

His eyes glittered with vivid yellow and dark green as he

stared at me.

"So, human. Are you stupid like the others?" he asked.

"No. And, my name is Mya."

He turned his gaze to Merdon.

"Why did you bring her here?"

"She was the one in the woods, Thallirin. The one Drav protects."

Oh, that didn't sound good. I blinked as I realized what woods he referred to. The moment outside McAlester when I'd had my pants down in the trees and an infected almost found me. I'd kissed Merdon by mistake. I stepped away from him, my eyes rounding.

"Hmm," Thallirin said as Merdon stepped toward me, a slight smile on his lips.

"You remember." Merdon crowded me, forcing me backwards until I hit the edge of the couch.

"Sit."

I sat and turned my head so I wouldn't be staring at his waist. I really didn't want to know what he thought of the kiss in the woods. Clasping my hands so they wouldn't shake, I reminded myself that the fey at Whiteman had been checking on me at regular intervals. When they found an empty kitchen, they would start looking. Hopefully, they'd find the pot by the fence and figure things out.

Merdon stepped aside, and Thallirin stalked closer.

"We want our exile lifted," Thallirin said.

"What?" I said. I'd heard him just fine. However, I didn't understand why he was talking to me about their exile.

"We want our exile lifted," he repeated, crossing his arms over his chest.

The cold, empty look in his eyes made my stomach churn. I swallowed with difficulty and tried to keep my voice from shaking.

"I don't know how to do that."

"I saw you with Drav," Merdon said. "He watches you. Carries you. Protects you. You are of importance to him. Even Molev consults you."

Thallirin leaned toward me, his hands braced against the back of the couch on either side of my head. His piercing gaze pinned me, and I tried not to shiver in fear.

"Are you important, Mya?"

"Yes," I whispered, afraid to lie. I was important in the way they were implying. Drav would do anything to get me back. That these two knew that terrified me.

Thallirin's gaze shifted between my two eyes.

"I see why. Your eyes beg me for mercy. For protection." He lifted a finger and gently brushed my cheek. "So soft and fragile. I would want to protect you, too."

He straightened away from me suddenly.

"Breathe, Mya. We mean you no harm."

I exhaled shakily and tried to muster some courage.

"I'm not sure I believe you. Molev exiled you because you killed someone. I don't think he's going to change his mind."

When Merdon growled something in their language, I wished I'd kept my mouth shut. Thallirin, however, didn't seem upset. He sat in the stuffed chair near me, the furniture creaking under his weight.

"That is why you are here. To listen when they would not." His gaze never wavered from mine. "Will you listen, Mya?"

I nodded jerkily. I'd listen to whatever he wanted and give

the fey time so they could find me.

"We are not the dangerous criminals they think us to be," Thallirin said. He leaned back in the chair and considered me for a moment. "Merdon saw Drav take you to the entrance of our home. You saw the glowing rocks in our world, yes?"

I nodded again.

"They give light and life, like this one." He lifted his wrist and showed me his crystal bracelet. "My first memory is of the caves and holding this crystal I now wear. I knew how to speak but didn't know my name or where I was. None of us did. That was our beginning.

"We started with nothing but the crystals we held and the seeds in our pouches. We worked hard, tying the crystals to our wrists to free our hands to help the plants grow. We spread out, working in small groups in the caves with the brightest crystals. We hunted to feed ourselves and wasted nothing because we had nothing."

He leaned forward, his gaze intense. "We planted. We hunted. We moved on. We did not know the monsters we were creating. You cannot imagine the confusion and desperation when the first hounds found us. We did not know what they were, only that they hunted us."

He exhaled heavily.

"It took time, and many deaths, to build the wall around our city. I was not the first reborn to the pool. But, I was the first to wonder how it worked. Why my clothes and hair did not return with me while my crystal did. No one else cared. The hellhounds were our priority."

"I tried not to care. I fought with the others to defend the wall and drive back the hounds. But with each death, I could not stop wondering why only the crystal always returned with us.

"After the wall was finished, Merdon, Oelm, and I went to the source where we harvested the larger crystals to keep the hounds away. As I worked, I kept wondering about the crystal on my wrist. I crushed my crystal, needing to see what would happen to me. Nothing happened. I felt no different. I cut myself and still healed quickly."

He looked down at his arm, lifting it enough to turn it to study the scars covering his skin. After a moment, he leaned back in his chair and focused on me again.

"Discouraged that I had been wrong about the crystal's importance to our rebirths, I went to retrieve a new one from the source. It gave me another, freely. It also filled my head with a vision of this world. Of killing a deer and waiting for it to come back to life."

"I saw that, too," I said, believing him. "When Drav brought me to your world, he wanted me to have a crystal. He thought it would work for me like it did for you, but the source didn't give me a crystal when I touched it. It gave me your history."

"And what did you see?"

I repeated the story the source crystal had shown me. He said nothing when I finished. His gaze stayed locked on the floor.

"What I don't understand is, why did it show me something instead of just giving me a crystal?"

"Because of our mistake." The anger in his eyes turned to bitterness.

"The crystal did not give me our history. Only the vision of the deer. And, I shared what the source crystal had shown me with Merdon and Oelm. All of us wondered what the vision meant. Oelm thought that the nearness of the crystals swayed the time it took to be reborn. He removed his crystal and told us to test his idea on him," he continued.

"And we did," Merdon said from behind me.

"When his body didn't leave, we tied the crystal back to his wrist. Still, his body remained. We carried him back to the city and placed him in the pool, but nothing happened. Oelm never returned, but we learned how important our crystals were. We were foolish to test the truth of the vision on our friend, and we were exiled because of it."

I couldn't deny that I felt a whole lot of pity for them. They'd made a huge mistake and had paid for it for a very long time. Why had the crystal shown Thallirin anything? Why had it shown me what it had? I looked at the floor, thinking.

"The crystal had been trying to warn you," I said, once again meeting his gaze. "At that time, you still didn't know the hounds were from the deer you ate, did you?"

"No. I believe the same as you. It was trying to tell us to stop killing the deer. We were too slow to understand that."

"I think the crystal was trying to warn me, too. My people are dying up here because of the hellhounds the fey accidentally created. The crystal changed you, giving you an immunity from the curse that created them. Humans don't have that immunity. I think the crystal was telling me that humans need the fey.

"It would have been easy for me to hate the fey for what'd been unleashed on my world had the crystal not shown me the truth. Now, I understand the fey had no choice about living in the caverns. I understand that none of you knew about the deer. I don't hate any of the fey for what's happened to my world."

I studied Thallirin for a minute, wondering what he would think of my next words.

"And while I agree that you made a mistake in killing your friend and have suffered long enough for it, I can't help but wonder if I should hate you for what you've done recently.

"You've been shooting out lights and letting the hellhounds and infected inside the fence to attack my people. Not just at the base where you stole me from, but also the first place we stayed."

Merdon growled, his fangs showing in his anger.

"They pierced our skin with their loud guns. They challenged us. It was our right to accept."

I considered both of them for a moment. They had no one to explain things to them. The other fey still wanted to remove heads when they were angry. Yet, they didn't because of me. These two had done no more than Drav had in the beginning. I could still remember the feeling of terror when the lights at the gas station had been broken the night I met Drav. Was I stupid to consider giving these two a chance to start over?

"Our ways are different. Gunfire isn't a challenge," I said. "It's a warning to stay away. We humans are just trying to survive, and we are afraid."

"Ah," Merdon said, calming.

"Yes. Ah. The rules are different up here. You can't behave the same way you did in the caves. What would you do if you were no longer exiled? What do you hope for?"

"To no longer be alone," Thallirin said.

"We miss our brothers," Merdon added.

The fey didn't have traditional families like humans, but they'd always had each other. Drav seemed to know each fey from his world and not just in passing. They were each other's family. I'd gone crazy trying to get back to mine. Why wouldn't it be the same for Thallirin and Merdon?

I studied the pair. Merdon stood by Thallirin's side. Both wore the same serious, forsaken expression. Both had more scars individually than I'd seen combined on all the other fey. They were fighters. Survivors. Like the rest of us. And, we humans needed as much help in this new world as we could get. Trading in an adversary for an ally made sense. Would Molev and Drav agree after I told them all of this?

They knew these men better than I did.

"You will speak on our behalf?" Thallirin asked, breaking the long silence.

"I will. But, you didn't help your case by stealing me. Drav is going to go crazy."

"But you will speak on our behalf," Merdon insisted. "There was no other way for us to speak with you."

"I will, but I can't guarantee it will help. Will you take me back to the base?"

"No. We will wait. Our brothers will come to us."

"That's probably not a wise plan. Your brothers would be more forgiving if you took me back."

Thallirin shook his head. "They would find us before we reached the fence and remove our heads before you could speak."

Given Drav's reaction when he found me at the school, Thallirin had a valid point.

225

"Fair enough. We'll wait. You wouldn't happen to have anything to eat, would you?" I asked.

"I do not know. We have not been here long."

"Mind if I look?"

Merdon extended his hand in the direction of the kitchen.

Nodding my thanks, I stood and went to check the cabinets. Merdon and Thallirin followed, watching me. Finding nothing significant in the cupboards, I opened the fridge before quickly closing it. The power had obviously gone out long ago.

"Don't open that," I said with a gag and a cough.

Moving around the room, I opened a plain door and found the pantry. Inside, cans of pork and beans, tuna, and little snack packs of mac-n-cheese sat on the shelves.

"Jackpot," I called, grabbing the tuna for the fey and a can of pears and a tin of chicken for me.

"Take a seat," I said, re-emerging from the pantry. I gestured at the table when they didn't move. "It's okay to sit."

Merdon and Thallirin sat and only glanced at the cans I put before them.

"You guys aren't hungry?" I asked, already moving to find the can opener.

Neither answered. When I glanced up from my search through the drawers, they were frowning at the cans. They didn't know what the cans were.

I found the can opener and grabbed some spoons from the drawers before joining them at the table. I reached over, picked up Merdon's can, and slowly opened it for him.

"It's tuna," I said. "A kind of meat that we've preserved." I started opening Merdon's can. "Most cans have something edible inside of them, but not all cans are meant for humans."

I set Merdon's can before him then gave them their spoons.

"I know you guys have rules about eating first based on the length of your hair. It's not like that here. You can go ahead and eat," I said, peeling the lid back on my chicken. After I took my first bite, they did the same.

"So, what have you been doing up here?" I asked after swallowing.

The two exchanged looks.

"We have been exploring," Merdon said.

"And killing?"

"We did not know there would be no rebirths," Merdon said, frustration lacing his words.

"You saw our home," Thallirin said. "You saw the safety the wall provided. Without that wall, the hounds hunted us. Merdon and I died countless times. Though we were strong fighters, stronger than those with longer hair, we were also tired.

"After the caves opened, we ran. We thought only of finding a place without the hounds. It was dark and strange. When we saw your people, they either wanted to bite us or use their guns. We accepted each challenge and removed many heads. But we never stayed to see their rebirth. Exile taught us to move. Fight. Stay alert."

"When did you realize we don't come back?" I asked.

"The birds in the sky killed many. No one returned," Merdon said.

"How did you learn English?"

"We watched and listened. One large, red home had a TV. We listened for one night and watched the men inside the fence shoot the stupid ones."

"They're starting to get less stupid," I said.

Thallirin nodded.

"We put something by the fence, and the less stupid ones climbed over the top. While the men were busy, we took the TV. It did not talk again, though," Merdon said.

"Yeah, TVs need electricity."

Thallirin nodded and set his spoon down by his empty can. I finished my chicken and started in on the pears.

"They come," Thallirin said, standing.

A moment later, a distant roar echoed outside.

TWENTY-ONE

My heart started beating faster, and I stood. Merdon wrapped his hand around my arm to stop me from rushing out the door.

"Will you speak for us?" Thallirin asked.

"I said I would."

"Then wait. If you leave, they will kill us."

"Mya," a voice yelled. Not Drav's, but one of the other fey's.

"I won't leave," I promised. "But they need to see me to believe I'm okay."

Merdon looked at Thallirin, who nodded. Merdon let me go, and I ran to the door and pulled it open.

"Drav," I called.

"Mya." The chorus of my name spoken by many voices spread out in the nearby woods.

"I'm here," I yelled. "I'm safe."

An infected stumbled out of the trees, its cloudy gaze finding me. It opened its mouth and moaned, sprinting toward me. Merdon pulled me back, and Thallirin rushed past us to meet the infected on the porch. The wet spray of its blood as Thallirin removed its head hit me across the face. I blinked and wiped the wetness away.

"I am sorry, Mya," Thallirin said, tossing the head to the side. "I could not allow it to harm you."

"No, it's okay. You can take the heads off the stupid ones. Just be careful with the infected blood around other humans. I don't know if the infection spreads in ways other than a bite."

He nodded and came back inside to stand behind me.

Further away, several big, gray bodies burst from the woods.

"Trust me," I said before stepping out onto the porch. The headless body of the infected lay not far from my feet when I stopped.

"I'm okay," I called again.

Molev ran at the front of the group, his expression a mix of anger and worry. More fey spilled from the trees as the first group passed.

From the other side of the clearing, another fey broke free of the woods and sprinted toward me. He ran so fast, he looked like a streak of gray, and I knew who it was before he reached me.

"Drav," I breathed.

Within seconds, he reached the porch and held me so tightly I could barely breathe.

"Mya," he said into my hair. "I will not let you out of my sight again. Never again, Mya."

"Too tight, Drav. I need to breathe."

His hold loosened, and he pulled back enough to cup my face and stare into my eyes.

"You gave your word."

I'd expected anger but not the pain in his eyes.

"I did, and I didn't break it. I swear. I want to tell you what happened, but first, I need you to promise me something." My gaze flicked to Molev and the rest of the fey who now surrounded the porch. "I need you all to promise me that you will listen and not do anything until I finish my story."

The hurt faded from Drav's eyes, replaced by worry. He released me and gently wiped my cheek. His finger came away with blood on it.

"Are you hurt, Mya?"

"No. I promise I'm not. That's infected blood. From that guy there," I said, pointing at its body.

Drav's gaze flicked to where I pointed. He frowned at the dead infected then focused on me.

"You did not do that," Drav said, softly. "Who is here with you?"

I shivered at the menace in his voice and looked at Molev for help.

"Do you promise to listen?"

Molev hesitated before giving me a single nod. I met Drav's angry gaze and put my hand on his chest. He shook beneath my touch.

"Do you promise?" I asked.

"I will listen. Then, I will react."

That didn't sound good. I took a deep breath and got to the point.

"Merdon and Thallirin are inside—"

Shouts filled the air from many of the fey who stood on the lawn. Molev and Drav looked murderous.

"—and I'd like you and Molev to come in with me so that I can tell you the story," I said loudly to be heard.

"No, Mya," Drav said.

"You promised."

"You do not understand."

"Maybe you're right. Maybe I don't. But, can you honestly say you understand when you haven't yet listened to what I have to say?"

He closed his eyes for a moment, exhaling deeply. I stood on my toes and gently touched my lips to his. His hands captured my head, cradling me gently as I lightly licked his lower lip.

"I need you to listen," I whispered against his mouth.

He sighed heavily and released me.

"I will listen."

I smiled and took his hand. He didn't budge when I tugged, though.

"I go first, my Mya."

He shared a look with Molev then led the way into the house.

Thallirin sat in the chair facing the door. Merdon stood beside him, leaving the couch empty. I quickly took the seat nearest Thallirin, ignoring Drav's growl, and patted the cushion beside me.

Drav sat. Molev stood. It was enough. For the next fifteen minutes, they listened.

"They made a mistake, and it cost a friend his life," I reiterated after I finished my tale. "They've paid for that mistake. We're in a different world now. A different world with different rules."

Drav's thumb, which had been exploring the back of my hand as I spoke, stilled.

"They stole you from me," he said, his voice dangerously

soft.

"Only because you left them with no other choice."

"I will not lift your exile," Molev said.

"Hang on, Molev."

"No, Mya. We have heard your story, and I deny their request."

I glanced at Thallirin and Merdon, who hadn't yet said a word. The cold, emptiness in their gazes made me afraid for our future. If I couldn't find a way to end their exile, I knew that the hellhounds would no longer be our biggest threat.

Taking a settling breath, I focused on Molev.

"Justice has been served. Thallirin and Merdon took a life and have lost their own countless times. More than any other fey. Exile for life, when your lives never end, is not justice. It's cruel," I said.

"You would have us welcome them back? Men who callously disregarded the safety of their closest friend?"

"No," I said.

Merdon growled in frustration.

"If you welcomed them back now, you would resent them and never trust them. What I'm asking is that you give them a chance to redeem themselves in your eyes. A chance, that's all."

"What do you suggest they do that would make up for the life they took, Mya?"

I looked at Merdon and Thallirin, taking in their scars and battle-hardened expressions, and hated what I was about to say.

"They each have to kill ten hellhounds. If they want to rejoin the fey and live with humans, they need to show they are willing to fight to protect us. They need to help give humans a chance at life."

Molev remained silent. He glanced over at Drav then at the two exiles.

"The fey are the only ones who can kill the hellhounds," I continued. "Each dead hound is one less threat to the humans who still live. These two would be saving lives as well as risking their own."

I could see the moment I began to sway Molev. He wasn't happy about it, but he understood the challenge the two fey would face.

"Do you agree to these terms?" Molev asked the exiles.

Thallirin stood, his expression set.

"I agree."

Merdon scowled but nodded.

"I as well."

"Remove their hearts and bring them back whole. I will witness you destroy them and count each heart as one kill," Molev said.

My heart ached for Merdon and Thallirin as Molev turned and left. I'd thought ten hearts a piece harsh. Bringing the hearts back whole meant the hellhounds wouldn't be dead. The creatures would likely be chasing the exiles the whole way back to Molev.

The determination in Merdon and Thallirin's eyes spoke volumes, though.

"The hounds won't die until the heart is crushed," I said, making sure they understood.

"But, it is a chance for us to come out of exile. Thank you, Mya," Merdon said, inclining his head.

"Thank you, sister," Thallirin said.

I stood, Drav shadowing me.

"When will you two leave?" I asked.

"Now. We wish to rejoin our people, and yours, as soon as possible."

With a nod to Drav, they walked out the door and down the steps. The fey outside parted for them but did not speak to them.

Drav wrapped his arms around my waist and pressed his nose into my hair.

"Does this mean you're not mad at me?" I asked, hopefully.

"I thought I lost you again, my Mya."

"Never, Drav. I will never leave you if I can help it."

He sighed gustily. "When Shax told me you had disappeared again, I feared the worst."

I turned in his arms and looked up at him.

"When Merdon picked me up and jumped over the fence, I should have been more scared than I was. Do you know why I wasn't?"

He shook his head.

"Because you will never let anything happen to me. Because I'm yours, and you're mine. And because you really, really like it when I jiggle."

He grinned and scooped me into his arms, pressing a dangerously hot kiss to my lips.

I wrapped my arms around his neck and let him have his way. When we finally broke apart, I could only think of one thing.

"Drav, take me home."

EPILOGUE

I watched Molev, Kerr, and Drav work with Ryan to get the solar panel they'd raided onto the roof of our house. An ice storm two days ago had cut power to our little community away from Whiteman. Some folks had called it quits and returned to Whiteman on the following supply run. Not us. Not the fey.

Ryan and Dad had started going out with them to collect what we needed to be "off the grid." Not that there was much of a grid anymore. Power failures were happening all over the place. Lack of people to maintain it, I supposed. And there were more infected to wreck things.

But, not here. It seemed that the infected had gotten smart enough to avoid the fey because they no longer wandered the area around our community. Or maybe they just didn't like the "wall" the fey had constructed around us. However, the scarcity of nearby infected meant that the fey went further afield on their hunting parties to kill infected and search for hellhounds.

"When's the next hunting party?" I asked.

"Tomorrow," Molev answered. "You will have heat before we leave."

"Go inside, Mya and Mom. It is too cold for you," Drav

called down.

"That's why we have winter jackets," I called back. "We're fine."

Mom chuckled.

"He is such a sweetheart. Do you know he wouldn't let me drive the tractor around the field because I was too jiggly on it? He didn't think your father would like the attention it was drawing."

I shook my head without taking my eyes from Drav. He wore jeans and a jacket like the rest of the fey, looking fairly human except for the grey skin still exposed on his hands and face.

"They sure do get fixated on body parts," I agreed.

"Just the girl ones."

I glanced at Mom, caught her wide grin, and got suspicious.

"What happened?"

"Ghua came to talk to me after I got off the tractor and said you told him to go away."

"Oh, God." I already knew where this was going and why I'd told him to go away.

"He was lamenting that fact when your father came up from behind him to hear, 'When will I get to see some pussy for myself?'"

I covered my face with my hands.

"Your father's reaction wasn't so mild. He got right in front of poor Ghua and hit him in the face. Then he lectured every fey within earshot about how it's inappropriate to talk about the p-word with a married woman."

I looked at Mom. "And they listened?"

Mom's smirk told me they hadn't. She opened her mouth

to say something, but her gaze shifted to someone approaching behind me. I looked over my shoulder at Ghua. His face looked remarkably unscathed.

"Good morning, Mom. Is Dad's hand feeling better?"

"It is, sweetie. Thank you for asking."

He nodded and looked at me.

"Mya, may I ask you something?"

"Sure. What's up?"

"Is every vagina the same or are they slightly different like our cocks?"

Mom busted out laughing.

"Fixated," she managed between hoots of laughter.

"Ghua, you need a hobby," I said.

"I did not use the p-word," he said, worriedly.

"You're fine, honey," Mom said with a pat on his arm. "Why don't you show me how your solar panel looks?"

Our roof wasn't the only roof getting a solar panel and some new wiring. Not only were the fey working to kill the hellhounds and infected during their rotations at Whiteman, they were also settling in to stay. Each fey had his own home that he was preparing in hopes of one day sharing it with a female.

Mom and Ghua walked two houses down to look over what Ghua had done. I could hear Mom's praise for his hard work.

The fey had a hard path before them, like the rest of us. During the day, the infected still caused a very real threat for any human away from the fey. At night, the hellhounds roamed, threatening both human and fey. But, I held onto hope, like the rest of the survivors.

It would take time and effort to rebuild a world together. But, with Drav, the fey, and my family at my side, I didn't fear the future. I welcomed it.

AUTHOR'S NOTE

What a ride! We loved writing this trilogy and hope to continue writing in this world and sharing stories for the rest of the guys. (We're already plotting for Shax and Ghua.)

Your support keeps us writing! Please tell other readers about these books or leave a review to spread the word about a story you loved or hated. Books with more reviews have more visibility on retailer sites, so each review counts!

If you want to keep up to date on our release news, teasers, and special giveaways, please consider subscribing to our newsletters. (We only send periodically, so you won't be overwhelmed.)

Until next time!

Melissa and Becca

ALSO BY MJ HAAG

Beastly Tales
Depravity
Deceit
Devastation

Lutha Chronicles
Escaping the Lutha
Facing the Lutha

Connect with the author
Website: MJHaag.MelissaHaag.com
Newsletter: MJHaag.MelissaHaag.com/subscribe

ALSO BY BECCA VINCENZA

Rebirth Series
Damaged
Healed
Stolen

Merc Series
Freelance
Contracted

Hexed Hearts
Hunters Heart

Connect with the author
Website: BeccaVincenzaAuthor.wordpress.com